'They're forgeries.

'You know perfectly well
to your pretty neck in all t

'I'm not up to my neck in anything.' Elena
wanted to scream.

'You are. But there is a way for you to save
yourself. And your father. And that is what I
mean about you posing a dilemma for me.'

'Go on.'

'The lack of evidence to support my innocence is
a setback for me.'

'That's because it doesn't exist.'

'If I'm such a master forger, don't you think
I would fake it?' Gabriele demanded. 'Your
father is a meticulous record-keeper. It's out
there somewhere and I *will* find it… Or I could
be persuaded to forget the whole thing. With
the right incentive I could also be persuaded to
destroy the evidence I copied last night rather
than pass it on.'

'What incentive are you talking about?' she
asked, her anger leaching out to be replaced with
wariness.

A smile curved his handsome face. 'That, you
will find, is the crucial question. To secure a
he   l   f   f   f   h   l   l   t of
yo   mple
th

Wedlocked!

Conveniently wedded, passionately bedded!

Whether there's a debt to be paid,
a will to be obeyed or a business to be saved…

She's got no choice but to say, 'I do!'

But these billionaire bridegrooms have got another
think coming if they think marriage will be easy…

Soon their convenient brides become the object
of an *inconvenient* desire!

Find out what happens after the vows in

Untouched Until Marriage
by Chantelle Shaw

The Billionaire's Defiant Acquisition
by Sharon Kendrick

One Night to Wedding Vows
by Kim Lawrence

Expecting a Royal Scandal
by Caitlin Crews

Look out for more **Wedlocked!** stories
coming soon!

WEDDED, BEDDED, BETRAYED

BY
MICHELLE SMART

First Published in Great Britain 2016
By Mills & Boon, an imprint of HarperCollins*Publishers*
1 London Bridge Street, London, SE1 9GF

© 2016 Michelle Smart

ISBN: 978-0-263-91621-8

Our policy is to use papers that are natural, renewable and recyclable
products and made from wood grown in sustainable forests. The logging
and manufacturing processes conform to the legal environmental
regulations of the country of origin.

Printed and bound in Spain
by CPI, Barcelona

Michelle Smart's love affair with books started when she was a baby, when she would cuddle them in her cot. A voracious reader of all genres, she found her love of romance established when she stumbled across her first Mills & Boon book at the age of twelve. She's been reading (and writing) them ever since. Michelle lives in Northamptonshire with her husband and two young Smarties.

Books by Michelle Smart

Mills & Boon Modern Romance

The Russian's Ultimatum
The Rings That Bind
The Perfect Cazorla Wife

The Kalliakis Crown

Talos Claims His Virgin
Theseus Discovers His Heir
Helios Crowns His Mistress

Society Weddings

The Greek's Pregnant Bride

The Irresistible Sicilians

What a Sicilian Husband Wants
The Sicilian's Unexpected Duty
Taming the Notorious Sicilian

Visit the Author Profile page at
millsandboon.co.uk for more titles.

This book is for Renata—
thanks for feeding my coffee addiction! xxx

CHAPTER ONE

THE SCREAM PIERCED through the silence of the Nutmeg Island chapel.

Gabriele Mantegna, having just climbed up the stairs from the basement, came to an abrupt halt.

Where the hell had that come from?

He switched off his torch, plunging the chapel into complete darkness, and listened hard.

Had that been a *woman's* scream? Surely not? Tonight, only the armed security crew inhabited the island.

Closing the basement door carefully, he walked to the one small window of the chapel not made of stained glass. It was too dark to see anything but after a moment a faint light appeared in the distance. It came from the Ricci house where at that moment an armed gang were helping themselves to all the priceless works of art and antiquities.

The island's security crew were blind to the gang, their monitors remotely tampered with and feeding them falsehoods.

Gabriele checked his watch and grimaced. He'd been on the island ten minutes longer than planned. Every extra minute increased his chances of getting caught. To reach the beach on the south side of the island, from where he would swim to safety, was a further ten-minute walk.

But he hadn't imagined the scream. He couldn't in good conscience make his escape without checking it out.

Swearing under his breath, Gabriele pushed open the heavy chapel door and stepped out into the warm Caribbean air. The next time Ignazio Ricci decided on a spot of peace and contemplation, he would find the code for the chapel alarm scrambled.

For a building designed for peaceable contemplation and worship, the Ricci chapel had been desecrated by Ignazio's real purpose.

It had all been there, directly beneath the chapel altar, in a basement stuffed with files dating back decades. A secret trail of blood money, the underbelly of the Ricci empire, hidden from the outside world. In the short time Gabriele had been in the basement he'd uncovered enough evidence of illegal dealings to have Ignazio spend the rest of his life in prison. He, Gabriele Mantegna, would personally hand the copied incriminating documents to the FBI. He would be there every day of the trial, seating himself so that Ignazio, the man who'd killed his father, would not be able to avoid seeing him.

When the judge's sentence was pronounced Ignazio would know that it was *he* who had sent him down.

But everything wasn't sunshine yet. The most important evidence for Gabriele, the documents that would have cleared his own name and exonerated his father once and for all, had not been found.

The evidence existed. He would find it if it took him the rest of his life.

Putting the missing evidence from his mind, Gabriele set out into the thick canopy of trees and, crouching low, made his way to the Ricci house, a huge villa set over three levels.

Lights shone from a downstairs window. Any subterfuge by the gang had been abandoned.

Something had gone wrong.

The men in the house were led by a criminal mastermind who went by the moniker of Carter. Carter's specialisation was in purloining high-end goods for order. Ming vases. Picassos. Caravaggios. Blue Diamonds. There wasn't a security system in the world, so the legend went, that Carter couldn't crack. He also had a knack of knowing where the shadier elements of high society kept their even shadier valuables, the type of valuables the owner most certainly would not report to the authorities. Carter took those items for himself.

The front door had been left ajar.

As he approached it, voices could be heard, muffled but undeniably angry.

Knowing he was taking a huge risk but unable to rid himself of the sound of the scream ringing in his ears, Gabriele pressed himself against the outside wall of the window nearest the front door, took a breath, and turned to look inside.

The main reception room was empty.

He pushed the door open a few more inches.

The muffled argument continued.

He crossed the threshold. The instant his neoprene dive slipper trod onto the hard lacquered wood flooring, a squeak rang out.

Swearing under his breath, Gabriele tried another step, placing his whole foot down in one tread. This time there was no squeak.

He took stock of his surroundings. The reception room had three doors. Only one, directly opposite him, was open.

He crossed cautiously, wishing there were at least a life-size statue to hide behind if needed. Reaching the door, he peered through it, taking in the wide cantilevered stairs to his right and craning his ears to the left in an attempt to determine what the men were arguing about. If it was a simple heist-gone-wrong scenario he would return to his plan and get the hell off this island.

But that scream...

It had definitely sounded feminine.

The arguing voices were all male. He still couldn't decipher what they were arguing about. He needed to get closer.

Before he could take another step, heavy footsteps treaded down the stairs. A huge figure dressed entirely in black strode past the door Gabriele was hiding behind and joined the others. He must have opened the door widely because now everything they said echoed off the great walls.

'The little cow bit me,' he said in an English accent, sounding incredulous.

'You didn't hurt her?' said another voice, this one American.

'Not as much as I'm going to when we get her out of here.'

'She's not going anywhere. We're leaving her here,' said the other voice sharply.

'She's seen my face.'

Much swearing ensued before the first man cut through the noise. 'I would still take her even if she couldn't identify me—whoever she is, she's got to be worth something and I want a slice of it.'

All the men started speaking at once, making it impossible to distinguish their words but the gist of it was clear enough. Upstairs was a woman, probably bound, and these men were arguing over what to do with her.

Suddenly the original man came storming back out, yelling over his shoulder, 'You pansies can debate it all you want. That bitch is mine and she's coming with us.'

The door was slammed shut behind him and the man hurried back up the stairs, taking a right turn at the top.

This was Gabriele's chance.

Not pausing to consider his options, he strode to the stairs then climbed them three at a time.

Half a dozen doors lined the hallway he found himself in but only one of them was open.

He peered cautiously inside.

The man stood in the middle of a pale blue bedroom, his back to him. Before him, her hands tied at the wrists to a headboard, her mouth gagged, her knees raised tightly to her chest, was a woman with terror-filled eyes.

Not giving the man time to respond, Gabriele stepped behind him and struck him in the neck, aiming for the spot that would bring instant unconsciousness. He aimed correctly. The man collapsed immediately, Gabriele only just catching him at the waist before he could fall in a thump to the floor and alert the men waiting below.

Laying him down carefully, he checked his pulse.

Satisfied he hadn't killed him, he unzipped the waterproof pouch and pulled out his penknife.

The woman's eyes widened further and she pulled her legs even closer to her chest, whimpers coming from behind the gag.

He crouched beside her.

'I'm not going to hurt you,' he said quietly, speaking in English. 'Do you understand what I'm saying?'

She whimpered some more but managed to nod.

There was something familiar about her...

'I need you to trust me. I am not with those men,' he said. 'If they hear you scream they will come up here and probably kill us both. I'm going to untie you and remove your gag and we're going to escape but I need your word you won't scream. Do I have your word?'

Another nod. The whimpering had stopped, the terror in her clear green eyes lessening a fraction. Now her eyes searched his, the familiarity he felt clearly reciprocated.

'We're going to escape,' he repeated. He sat on the side of the bed and lifted her head, enabling him to untie the cloth that had been wrapped around her mouth. As soon as it was freed, he placed a finger to her lips. 'We don't have much time,' he warned. 'We're going to have to escape through a window unless you know a way out that doesn't involve going downstairs?'

She jerked her head to an interconnecting door behind her. 'The dressing room is above a roof. We can slip out through the window in there.' Her husky voice was croaky. He guessed the scream she'd given had damaged her vocal cords. He could only hope she hadn't suffered damage of any other kind.

He admired the fact that through the abject terror she'd just experienced, she'd still had the foresight to plan an escape route in her head.

He thought of Paul, the captain of his yacht, who would soon be on the lookout for his return.

'Give me one moment,' he said, pulling his phone out of his pouch and pressing the emergency button that would connect him.

'Paul, I need the jet ski to be brought to the north harbour immediately.' It was one of the many contingency plans they had spent two days running through. Gabriele attempting one of these contingency plans with a woman in tow hadn't been in any of the blueprints.

His call done with, he sliced his penknife through the ropes binding the woman and quickly pulled the lengths away from her. Dark red welts encircled her wrists where the man had cruelly tied the rope so it bit into her tender flesh.

A groan came from the floor.

Gabriele ignored the urge to throw himself on the prostrate man and kick him in the ribs. Avenging this woman might give fleeting satisfaction but they could not afford to waste a single moment.

'Can you walk?' he asked, wrapping an arm around her waist and helping her sit up.

The woman was tiny. With white-blonde hair tied in a messy ponytail and those large green eyes, she reminded him of a porcelain doll. Breakable.

She nodded, but allowed him to help her to her feet. He wrinkled his nose. She smelt like a…bonfire? Studying her in more depth, he revised his porcelain doll opinion and altered it to grubby urchin.

Suddenly it came to him why she looked so familiar.

He recalled a small, doll-like girl from his youth, who had dressed like a boy and been able to climb a tree faster than anyone and then shimmy back down it as if a twenty-foot drop was nothing to worry about.

This was Ignazio's only daughter, Elena.

He was putting his life at risk for his enemy's daughter?

This woman was his enemy every bit as much as her father was. When Gabriele brought Ignazio's downfall he had every intention of bringing his entire family down with him.

The man on the floor's groans were becoming louder. Elena was eyeing him with a look that suggested she very much wanted to kick him in the ribs too.

'We need to leave now.' Gabriele grabbed her hand, having the presence of mind to avoid her wrists, and tugged her away and through to the dressing room she'd spoken of.

Whatever his personal feelings towards her and her family, and his plan to destroy them all, his destruction did not include allowing a vulnerable woman to be at the mercy of four armed men, one of whom he'd heard with his own ears wanted to hurt her.

He might hate Elena's family but he still wouldn't abandon her to such a fate.

He pulled the sash window up and looked out. As she'd said, a sloping roof ran under it.

Gabriele heaved himself out, dropping a couple of feet onto the roof.

'Come,' he said, righting himself when he was certain the roof was stable enough to hold his weight without crumbling beneath him.

Elena was already hoisting herself over the ledge. He put his hands to her tiny waist and helped her out, holding her tightly until he was sure she was secure on the roof. Apart from her bare feet, she was dressed in the perfect attire for escape, in long black shorts and a baggy khaki T-shirt.

Without exchanging a word, they both shimmied down to the edge of the roof.

'Rescue is coming from the north beach,' he said as he

tried to get his bearings as to where they were, exactly, in conjunction with said beach. 'We need to run to the right.'

She nodded, grim determination on her face, and then expertly swung over the edge so she was holding onto the rim of the roof with her fingers.

Being much larger, it took Gabriele a little longer to drop down. Before he could let go, she'd released her hold and fallen onto the wraparound veranda. Immediately she was back on her feet and jumping over the wooden rail and running to safety...except she was running to the left of the beach and not the right as they'd agreed.

He let go. He landed heavily but ignored the pain that shot up his leg and set off after her, calling as loudly as he dared, 'You're going the wrong way.'

She didn't look back. The band holding her hair back had come out, her long, straight white-blonde hair billowing behind her.

Run, Elena, run.

In her mind's eye she pictured the tree house her father's staff had built for her and her brothers when they'd been children. If she could only reach it undetected, she would be safe.

But no matter how quickly she ran along the beach, she could hear him gaining on her.

Gabriele Mantegna. A man she vaguely remembered from her childhood. A man who scared her as much as the armed men in her family's holiday home.

This was the man who had spent two years in an American federal prison and tried to implicate her father in his criminality.

In the distance ahead was the pathway that led into the forest and to her sanctuary.

She pushed on even harder but still he gained ground. His breaths were heavy behind her.

She wasn't going to make it.

A burst of fury rent through her, overriding her fear. She would not allow herself to be captured by this man.

Coming to an abrupt halt, she turned on the spot and charged, propelling her entire body at him. It was like charging at a brick wall.

But her ruse worked. Taken by surprise, Gabriele stumbled back onto the sand. Unfortunately he wasn't so off guard that he didn't immediately hook his foot around her ankle, sending her tumbling on top of him. Within seconds he had gained the upper hand, twisting her onto her back and pinioning her beneath him.

'Are you trying to get yourself killed?' he demanded, his angry breath hot on her face.

Bucking beneath him, she tried everything she could to throw him off but she was too tightly caught.

Gabriele swore and, panther-like, sprang back to his feet. There was no way for her to escape again for he unceremoniously pulled her up, hooked an arm around her waist, and slung her over his shoulder.

No sooner had he started running than shouts echoed from the house.

Terror as she had never experienced, not even when she'd unexpectedly stumbled upon the gang, careered through her.

Yet, even with the indignity of being carried like a naughty child and the pain in her stomach as it jostled against his shoulder, when the first gun shots rang out she squeezed her eyes shut and thanked God for Gabriele's strength, and prayed for the shots to fire wide.

She had no idea how long he ran with her thrown over his shoulder. It could have been one minute, it could have been an hour. All she knew was that the men were chasing and firing at them.

And then he was no longer running with her on the sand but wading through the sea. An engine ran close by. She hardly had time to register that a jet ski had appeared from nowhere before Gabriele had climbed onto it and shouted, 'Go!'

Whoever was driving didn't need telling twice. The jet ski shot off over the still waters.

Somehow Gabriele manipulated her body so she was no longer draped over his shoulder but secured on his lap, sandwiched between him and the man riding the jet ski.

Within minutes they approached an enormous yacht. To Elena's amazement, they steered straight into an opened hatch on the side and parked, exactly as if they were parking a car in a garage.

Gabriele and the man who'd ridden the jet ski helped her off.

'Are you all right?' Gabriele asked, looking at her closely.

She opened her mouth to retort defiantly that of course she was all right when the magnitude of everything she'd gone through that evening and the exhaustion that had brought her to Nutmeg Island hit her.

A hot fog formed in her brain, perspiration breaking out all over, her hands suddenly clammy.

And then it all went black.

CHAPTER TWO

ELENA AWOKE TO find herself cocooned in a heavy duvet on a bed so comfortable that for a moment the fact she didn't have a clue where she was didn't matter.

She stretched then sat bolt upright as memories flooded her.

She'd fainted. She remembered feeling all…wrong, remembered strong arms holding her, overriding her protests.

Gabriele Mantegna .

He'd kidnapped her. He'd given chase, thrown her over his shoulder and spirited her to his yacht via a jet ski.

Or had he saved her?

Yes, that was right. He'd certainly saved her from the criminal gang who'd done the unthinkable and overridden her father's state-of-the-art security system and broken onto their island.

But he was Gabriele Mantegna and instinct told her she'd be no safer with him than those men. The danger he carried was of a different kind.

He'd carried her away from the hail of bullets that had rained on them. God alone knew how they'd escaped without being shot.

What was he even doing there?

So many thoughts crammed in her brain it was a struggle to think straight.

Another memory came to her, of being placed on the bed and Gabriele's rich voice murmuring in their native Italian that she should sleep.

The only comfort she could take was that her clothes were still on.

Climbing out of bed, she held onto the frame until she

was certain her feet were steady, then drew the floor-length curtains.

Light flooded the cabin, almost blinding her with its brilliance. She opened the French doors and stepped out onto the balcony. The Caribbean Sea—at least she assumed they were still on the Caribbean—was calm, the yacht powering through it at a remarkable rate. If she closed her eyes she wouldn't know they were sailing.

Movement behind her made her turn and find a woman dressed in a maid's outfit standing at the door of her cabin.

The maid gave a tentative smile. 'Good morning Signorina Ricci,' she said in Italian. 'Can I get you some breakfast?'

The sea air had done a good job of clearing Elena's head and reinvigorating her. As much as she wanted food and a hot shower, what she needed was to see Gabriele and find out what the hell was going on.

'I would like you to take me to Signor Mantegna.'

The maid nodded her acquiescence and Elena followed her out of the cabin and into a wide corridor. A flight of steps led into a huge atrium where a white grand piano sat in the centre ringed by a circle of plush white sofas.

Gabriele was found on the third deck, sitting at a table overlooking a large, oval swimming pool, eating from a bowl of fruit.

He rose to his feet. He wore only a pair of canvas shorts. 'Good morning, Elena. How are you feeling?'

'Much better thank you,' she replied coolly, feeling her cheeks flame as she remembered basically falling into a dead faint at his feet.

Being eye level with his naked chest only caused the flames to burn harder. Quickly, she averted her gaze.

'You gave us quite a scare. Please, sit down. Coffee? Food?'

She took the seat opposite him. 'A *caffe e latte* would be nice.'

Turning to the maid, he said, 'Esmerelda, a *caffe e latte* and a tray of pastries for our guest, and a fresh pot of coffee for me please.'

While he spoke to the maid, Elena took the opportunity to flash her eyes over him.

Last night Gabriele had been dressed in a black wetsuit. It had been obvious then that he had a good body on him. However, nothing could have prepared her for seeing it in the flesh. Strong and defined, it was covered across the pecs with fine dark hair. This, coupled with his deep bronze colour, was testament to a man who enjoyed the outside life.

But there had been a couple of years when his outdoor recreation would have been severely limited...

'What's going on?' she asked abruptly.

It wasn't as if she hadn't seen a topless man before, she reminded herself. She had three older brothers. The male physique was hardly a mystery.

'I appreciate you saved me from those men last night but what were you doing on our island? If you had nothing to do with those men, how did you know to rescue me?'

It could only have been for nefarious purposes. Ever since Gabriele's release from prison he'd been conducting a subtle one-man vendetta against her family. The media intrusion had become intolerable.

The handsome, charismatic billionaire head of Mantegna Cars, a convicted fraudster and money-launderer, never missed an opportunity to make digs at her father. Gabriele had pleaded guilty to the charges and taken sole responsibility—though it was widely believed he'd only done so to save his own father—but many whispers had reached the media that Gabriele was fingering Ignazio Ricci as the real culprit.

Thoughtful eyes, such a dark brown colour they appeared black, met her gaze. With his strong nose and wide, sensuous lips, Gabriele's features had a soulful quality that was totally incongruous for a man such as him.

'I heard you scream. That's how I knew there was someone in danger.'

Her throat still hurt from that scream.

'We'll wait until your refreshments have been served and then we can talk about the rest of it.' His gaze flickered over her, scrutinising her in a fashion that made her flush. Having not looked in a mirror, she could only imagine how awful she looked with her bed hair and the clothes she'd fished in, made a bonfire in and slept in.

'Can you at least tell me where we are?'

'We are currently in the Gulf of Mexico. All being well we should arrive at Tampa Bay by early evening.'

Since assuring himself that Elena's faint wasn't anything to worry about, Gabriele had done some research on the woman he hadn't set eyes on in over two decades. His mind had been so filled with revenge on Ignazio and, to a lesser extent, his three sons, he'd almost forgotten she existed.

From thinking a man like Ignazio didn't have the capacity to love anyone, Gabriele now knew that, in Elena, he had found his nemesis's Achilles heel.

Their fathers had been close friends since childhood. When Alfredo, Gabriele's father, had emigrated from Italy to the US with his wife and young son, their friendship had endured. Alfredo had passed on his new American contacts to Ignazio and vouched for him, enabling him to expand his own growing empire.

Their businesses had been complementary, with Ricci Components supplying many of the parts fitted in Mantegna Cars. Both men had subsequently diversified from their business origins and a decade ago had merged the overlapping aspects of their respective businesses, at Ignazio's suggestion. Gabriele had had some reservations about the merger but had kept them to himself—after all, Ignazio was practically family.

Despite their enduring closeness, Ignazio had kept his only daughter hidden away in Italy. Gabriele doubted he had seen Elena in the flesh more than a handful of times since she was a toddler. His only real memory of her was as an unabashed tomboy.

The light of her father's eye, she had been home educated and protected all her life. She'd joined her father's business at the age of eighteen and worked closely with him for a number of years before being given the role of running the European division of Ignazio's empire.

Unlike her brothers, who had all the subtlety of a trio of strutting peacocks, she still, as an adult, kept in the background. Media sightings of her were slim and those that existed were all business related.

One particular broadsheet interview with Ignazio had caught his attention. It had been conducted four years ago, when Gabriele's father had first been charged. Ignazio had slated Alfredo and spoken eloquently about how 'duped' he felt. The only sincere words Gabriele had sensed from the man had been about his daughter:

'Elena is the hardest worker of my staff and the best child a man could hope for. I know when I become infirm, she will be there to care for me.'

He allowed himself a smile.

Gabriele's visit to the Ricci chapel might not have provided the evidence to clear his name he so badly wanted but in Elena he had found a silver lining. He'd found a weapon that could hurt Ignazio much more than merely sending him to prison.

Oh, yes, as a weapon to hurt Ignazio, he had found none better.

But then his smile dropped.

There would be nothing to celebrate until he found the evidence that cleared his father's name—and his own—and would allow his mother whatever peace she was capable of finding.

'I should tell you that your presence here has presented me with something of a dilemma,' he said.

Her brows drew together, her startling green eyes holding his. 'What kind of dilemma?'

'You have provided me with options I hadn't considered before.' Seeing Esmerelda returning to them, he left it at that.

Elena's *caffe e latte,* a large fresh pot of coffee and a plate of pastries were placed between them, and Gabriele's coffee poured.

'Please, eat,' he instructed with a wave of a hand, as Esmerelda disappeared back inside.

'Tell me why I'm a dilemma.'

'I would prefer to have this conversation without worrying you're going to fall into another faint due to hunger.'

'I've never fainted before,' she stated matter-of-factly. 'It was the shock and adrenaline of everything, that's all. I've never been kidnapped before and then rescued, then chased, then thrown over a shoulder to a jet ski with live ammunition being fired at me.'

'Why did you run from me?' he asked curiously.

'Because you have a grudge against my father and hate my family. You appeared in the room like a dark phantom—I was scared.'

'I don't hold a grudge against your father,' he denied calmly. 'My loathing towards all you Riccis is much stronger than that.'

Her pretty, lightly golden face paled. 'Then why did you rescue me?'

'Because I'm not such a monster that I would leave you at the mercy of those men.'

A tiny, shaking hand took a cornetto. Instead of biting into it, she put it on the plate before her, then took a sip of her *caffe e latte.*

'I don't understand why you hate us all so much.'

'Really?' He allowed his disbelief to ring through the syllables. Elena was a child of Ignazio's loins. She worked closely with him. Gabriele doubted there was anything about Ignazio's business practices she was unaware of. She was as guilty as he. 'Then let me educate you.'

At the foot of the table sat his briefcase. He pulled it onto his lap, opened it, and took out a document file.

'I went to Nutmeg Island last night searching for evidence of your father's criminality. These are a few of the documents I copied from the basement of your family chapel last night. As you can see, I've had them printed off to make digesting them easier. These are irrefutable proof that Ricci Components is laundering money from its Brazilian base.'

'You're lying.' She bit into her cornetto. A small dollop of raspberry jam dripped down her chin. She wiped it away with a finger and licked it, all the while staring at him with eyes that had hardened.

'Read them for yourself,' he answered with a shrug. 'The proof is there. The US authorities will find it indisputable.'

Something flickered in her eyes.

'Your father's been running his business from Brazil for well over a decade. However, the accounts concerned use US dollars. That gives the US a jurisdictional right to launch an investigation. Trust me, should I give them these documents, they will be on your father and the rest of you like a pack of hyenas on a fresh carcass. Why do you think I spent only two years of a six-year sentence behind bars? They know your father's up to his neck in corruption but, until now, they've not had the evidence to charge him with anything.'

She swallowed her food and swiped a hand through her fringe, then snatched the file from him. Sipping her *caffe e latte*, she began reading through the papers.

Gabriele watched her closely. Her green eyes zoomed from left to right and back again, a concentration frown just noticeable beneath her fringe.

In the years since he'd last seen her, she'd gained a doll-like prettiness about her that, combined with her rather grubby appearance and boyish clothes, had the effect of making her appear younger than her twenty-five years. He had to remind himself that there was nothing doll-like or immature about her spine. She'd proved her tenacity last night: she'd had an escape route planned despite the terror that would have frozen any other person's brain, and not only had she run away from him but, when realising she couldn't outrun him, had fought back. If his own reflexes weren't so quick she would likely have escaped him.

But she would never have escaped the men. They would never have let her go. They couldn't have afforded to, not once she had seen her captor's face.

Whatever direction this conversation took, he could not afford to let those big green eyes beguile him into thinking she was something less than she truly was.

'Whoever created these documents is clearly a master forger,' she said tightly when she'd finished reading.

'Don't fool yourself. They're not forgeries. I took the pictures myself last night, in your chapel basement.'

'Which you broke into.' Her eyes narrowed, more suspicion and distrust ringing from them. 'Were you in league with those men?'

'No.'

'So it's coincidence you were there at the exact same time an armed gang raided our holiday island?'

'No coincidence at all.' He gave a nonchalant shrug. 'I knew they would be making their heist. I've waited a year for it.'

She stared at him with a clenched jaw.

He allowed himself a smile. 'The thing you have to understand about prison is that it's full of criminals. Not all prisoners are discreet. One liked to brag about how his brother was a member of Carter's gang. Have you heard of Carter?'

She shook her head.

'Carter steals to order. His price tag for a job is reputed to be ten million dollars.'

She let out a low whistle.

'He also does jobs for himself—heists where he knows illegal artefacts are kept. The kind of stuff no owner would dare report stolen to the police.' Gabriele rested his elbows on the table and leaned forward. 'It was a simple matter to tell my fellow prisoner of the island off the Cayman Isles packed full of illegal art worth tens of millions of dollars.'

'That's a lie,' she snapped, finally showing some animation.

He shrugged. 'Carter didn't believe it to be a lie and he does meticulous research. I knew it was only a matter of time before word reached him. I've been keeping close tabs on him and waiting for his gang to make their move— I have to give credit to your father, his security system is second to none. I knew it would take the best to break it and Carter is the best. All I had to do was wait for him to make his move and use his gang as cover to enter the island undetected.'

Her green eyes flashed with contempt. 'So *you* brought those men to my family's island?'

'All I did was plant the idea.' He rubbed at his jaw. 'You weren't supposed to be there. No one was. Carter's got away with it for so long because he doesn't take unnecessary risks.'

'If you're so convinced of my father's guilt, why didn't you take the risk yourself? Why use a bunch of criminals as cover?'

He smiled without humour. 'I've already spent two years in prison. Believe me, I have no wish to spend another day there. I let the experts take the risk.'

Without warning, she jumped up from her chair and hurried to the railing, whereby she threw the file overboard. The papers flew out, the breeze lifting them and scattering them in all directions.

'That's what I think of your evidence,' Elena said coldly, trying desperately to hide the fact her heart was thrumming madly and her blood felt as if ice had been injected directly into her bloodstream.

This was all a horrible lie. There was no other explanation.

Her father was *not* a criminal. It was possible some of his art might not be entirely legitimate but illegal art was a world away from fraud and money laundering. He was a good, loving man who had raised her and her three older brothers single-handedly after her mother's death when Elena had been a toddler.

She watched Gabriele's jaw clench. He gripped hold of his coffee and downed it.

She hoped it scorched him.

'There is plenty more evidence,' he said in a tone far more even than the brimstone firing from his now black eyes portrayed. 'One phone call will be enough to have the FBI and the local police obtain a search warrant. One call. Would you like me to make it?'

'Why would they believe you?' she sneered. 'You're a convicted criminal and that "evidence" is illegally gained. It wouldn't stand up in any court.'

'It's enough to get the ball rolling. The authorities are watching your father. They're watching your brothers…and they're watching you. Your family is like a collection of kindling. All the authorities are waiting on is the match to light it. If the worst happens and they judge they can't use the evidence, then copies of the documents will be emailed from an anonymous, untraceable email address to every major news outlet in the world. Either way he's finished, and you're finished too.'

Elena put a hand to her chest and blinked hard to clear the clouds swimming in her eyes.

Whoever Gabriele had paid to create the documents was

a master of the art. Anyone looking at them could be forgiven for thinking they had an air of legitimacy to them.

Her father—her entire family—had been living under a cloud of suspicion for a year, ever since Gabriele had been released from prison and begun his whispering campaign against them. He'd been clever about it, always making sure his comments were right on the cusp of slandcrous.

There had been other incidents too, minor in the grand scheme of things; investors pulling out of deals at the last moment, the banks insisting on greater scrutiny of the books, all the little things that could be passed off as consequences of a turbulent global economy but as a whole were evidence of someone working against them.

She clung to the railing, her knuckles turning white. 'Do you hate us because my father never stood up for your father when the accusations first came out? Is that the reason for all this?'

He laughed. It was the bitterest sound she had ever heard.

'You're very good at the wide-eyed ingénue act, I'll give you that,' he said with a shake of his dark head. 'One could almost believe you're naïve about the fact that it was *your* father behind it all.'

She shook her head. 'You're lying. Everyone knows you and your father were in on it together. You took the rap to sparc him. My father was questioned *once* and they found no evidence against him.'

'They found no evidence against *your* father because the trail he made was deliberately laid to lead to *my* father,' he snarled, showing the first real sign of anger, enough to make her recoil and tighten her hold on the rail. 'The FBI has been trying to pin something on him for years. Our fathers went into business together at your father's instigation so he could hide behind my father's respectability. He used my father's affection, good nature and loyalty to an old friend, and framed him.'

'Where's the evidence? You're making a lot of nasty insinuations and accusations here but where's a shred of evidence to back up the claims?'

'It's out there and I will find it.'

'Or forge it like you did those other documents you claim are from the chapel basement.'

Her father had stored business documents in the chapel basement for decades. There was nothing sinister about it—it was simply the most secure place for them. Or, rather, had been.

'Admit it, Elena, the documents I copied last night are the real deal. Their release is the smoking gun the FBI is waiting for.'

'They're forgeries.' But she could not deny that they were brilliantly constructed forgeries. As far as forgeries went, they were perfect.

'You know perfectly well they're not. You're up to your pretty neck in all this.'

'I'm not up to my neck in anything.' She wanted to scream. This entire conversation was like something from Dante.

'You are. But there is a way for you to save yourself. And your father. And that is what I mean about you posing a dilemma for me.'

'Go on.'

'The lack of documentary evidence to support mine and my father's innocence is a setback for me.'

'That's because it doesn't exist.'

'If I'm such a master forger don't you think I would fake it?' he demanded. 'Your father is a meticulous record keeper. It's out there somewhere and I will find it…or I could be persuaded to forget the whole thing. With the right incentive I could also be persuaded to destroy the evidence I copied last night rather than pass it on.'

'What incentive are you talking about?' she asked, the anger leeching out to be replaced with wariness.

'I've held back from sending the documents to the FBI because I have a proposition to make. You and you alone can save your father from financial ruin and a hefty prison sentence.'

'What does this proposition entail?'

A smile curved his handsome face. 'That, you will find, is the crucial question. To secure a healthy future for your father and the rest of your family, you will have to do one very simple thing—you'll have to marry me.'

CHAPTER THREE

GABRIELE WATCHED CLOSELY as the blood drained from Elena's face, the light golden colour turning white. The last thing he wanted was her falling into a faint again, especially as there was no possibility of him catching her as he'd done the night before.

It was the last thing he should have worried about. Instead of falling into a heap on the floor, she covered her mouth and burst into peals of laughter. And not just a short burst of it. Her body shook, the colour flooding back in her face.

'That's the funniest thing I've ever heard,' she said, wiping away tears of mirth with the back of her hand. 'You want to marry me?'

He didn't say anything, just folded his arms across his chest and stared at her implacably.

She must have seen something in his expression for all merriment came to an abrupt halt.

'You don't mean it? Do you? You want to marry me?'

'Marry me and all your father's financial and legal problems disappear.'

'But... But that's insane.' She ran her fingers through her messy hair. 'Tell me what your real proposition is.'

'That's it. I want my ring on your finger and my baby in your belly.'

'A baby? You want me to have a *baby* with you? You *are* insane—'

'Those are my conditions for not throwing your father and the rest of your family to the mercy of the authorities.'

She shook her head, visibly pulling herself together. Dragging herself away from the railing, she rejoined him at the table, finished her *caffe e latte*, then helped herself to the fresh pot of coffee.

Done, she leaned forward, her fingertips holding onto the table as if they were suction pads.

'Putting aside the fact your proposition is the most stupid idea in the history of humanity, and putting aside your monstrous idea of us having a baby together, what would you hope to achieve by marrying me? My humiliation? My subjugation? *What?*'

'I have one mission in my life and that's your father's destruction. You marrying me...' he allowed himself the luxury of imagining Ignazio's reaction to the news '...will destroy him emotionally. You're his special princess; the light of his life. Knowing you belong to me will cut right into what is left of his heart.'

Her eyes flashed pure hatred at him. 'I will never belong to you. And I am *not* having your child.'

'If you agree to my proposition you will take my name. You will have my child. A Ricci will become a Mantegna. Together we will make a new life.' Now Gabriele leaned forward to mimic her stance, placing his fingers on the table so they almost touched hers. 'Your father, your brothers, the whole world will believe you have fallen in love with me and that whatever heart you have in your body belongs to me.'

Now her eyes were wide with stark panic. 'I can't do it. No one would believe we're in love for a second.'

He shrugged. 'It will be your job to make them believe it.'

She rubbed at her eyes. He looked closely to see if there were tears but clearly Elena, despite her doll-like exterior and unfortunate fainting fit, was tough. It wasn't a thought that should make him glad but it did.

Knowing she was more than equipped to be his equal lessened a fraction of the guilt trying to eat at him.

He would not allow himself to feel guilt. After what her father had done, guilt and empathy had no place in his life.

Gabriele's father had worked hard all his life, had been a loyal and faithful husband, father, employer and friend. To see his reputation trashed and the anguish it had caused, along with his father's bewilderment that the man he'd considered a brother had been the root of it all…

'It's one thing wanting to hurt my father but why are you dragging me into it?' she asked, shaking her head. 'I've done nothing to you. I don't even know you.'

'Because I know you're as guilty as he is. Even if you didn't have a direct hand in the framing of my father, you did nothing to stop it. Your father is a monster yet you act as if he were a deity. You should consider yourself lucky that I'm giving you this chance. Be in no doubt, the FBI will find evidence against you and your brothers too.' Gabriele rose from the table. 'I appreciate it's a lot for you to take in so I shall give you some time to think things through.'

'How long? How long, damn you?'

He looked at his watch. 'I want your decision by the time we reach Tampa Bay.'

'I can't…' She swallowed, her face pinched and furious. 'I can't. It's impossible.'

'You can. The choice will ultimately be yours. Just bear in mind that should you choose the wrong option, your father will spend what's left of his miserable life in a prison cell. There might even be a cell with your name on it too.'

As he walked back indoors, the feel of her hate-filled eyes burning into his back, he took some deep breaths to dislodge the uncomfortable, cramp-like feeling that had settled in his chest.

A hot shower made Elena feel cleaner but not at all better.

She'd sat outside on the deck for almost an hour, trying hard to think but being unable to drag up a coherent thought.

She should never have taken the long weekend off work.

She'd hardly taken any time off in the past year: since Gabriele had started his whispering campaign she hadn't dared. She'd wanted her employees and the Ricci shareholders to see her relaxed and unworried. An average week would see her travel to a minimum of four countries. Yes, she travelled by private jet but even thirty thousand feet in the air there was no respite to be had. Always there was paperwork to catch up on, emails to send and reply to, daily conference calls with her father.

A fortnight ago she'd caught a cold that wouldn't shift. As the days had passed her energy levels had sapped. Getting out of bed had become a feat of endurance. Then, on Thursday, she'd sat through a board meeting in Oslo fighting to keep her eyes open. As soon as it had finished she'd dragged herself into her office, sank onto the sofa and promptly fallen asleep. While she'd slept she'd dreamt of the family Caribbean island, bought two decades ago, and had woken knowing she needed a break. She didn't need a doctor to tell her she was in danger of burnout.

Their home on the island was big enough that all the family could come and go as they pleased. As a rule, they notified the household staff so preparations could be made, but on this fateful occasion she'd decided what she needed more than anything was peace. Just the thought of being completely alone—obviously with the exception of the unobtrusive security guards—had lifted her spirits.

Three days of solitude and sunshine…

She'd arrived on the island late yesterday afternoon. She'd dumped her case in the house and then decided to do something she hadn't done since she was a child, and head to the south of the island where the clear shallow waters allowed her to wade far out, and catch a fish for her supper.

Her belly rumbled as she recalled how she'd never had a chance to eat her catch, a juvenile foot-long barracuda.

The sun had gone down and she'd built a small fire on

the beach. Her barracuda had been almost cooked to perfection when shouts had distracted her.

She'd assumed one of the security guards had injured himself and rushed off through the woods to help.

Luck had not been on her side. She'd stepped onto the main drive that cut through the woods at the exact moment the man clad head to foot in black had stepped out of the house. He couldn't miss her.

She'd been rooted to the ground, her shock so great she'd been unable to move more than a muscle. It was as if her brain had been incapable of comprehending that there was a stranger before her and that this stranger represented danger.

Then the adrenaline had kicked in and she'd turned to run but by then it had been too late—the man had already yelled for back-up and was powering towards her. So she'd done the only thing she could. She'd opened her throat and screamed, literally, for her life.

Thank the Lord that Gabriele had heard it. She couldn't bear to think of what would have happened if he hadn't, or if he'd ignored it.

Her wrists were still sore from where that man had tied her to the bed. He hadn't cared if he hurt her. Indeed, she would guess he got off on it.

It was this knowledge, that Gabriele had put himself in danger to rescue her, that tempered the fury ravaging her entire body. Even her *toes* were angry.

But he *had* saved her. He'd put himself in grave danger for her. When he'd slung her over his shoulder there had been an understandable impatience but not a roughness. Hurting her had been the last thing on his mind.

A bitter laugh flew from her mouth. She'd bet he wouldn't have bothered coming to her rescue if he'd known that it was *she* who was in danger.

Or maybe he would have.

Saving her had presented him with an opportunity and he was grabbing it with both enormous hands.

It felt as if needles were being pushed into her scalp and forehead.

She couldn't marry him. She'd never heard such a ridiculous notion in her life. Marrying a man she barely knew and who was intent on destroying her entire family?

And to have his child? To bring a child into such a hate-filled nest of poison?

Yet it was the only way to save her family. Those forged documents had the potential to destroy them all and she was the only one who could stop it happening.

No wonder her head hurt so much.

Forcing herself to gather her wits, Elena hunted around the cabin for something clean to wear as Esmerelda had whisked her filthy clothes away. All she found was a white silk robe hanging in the wardrobe. It felt beautiful on her skin but one look in the mirror made her whip it off. The material was practically transparent.

Esmerelda had brought some clothes for her to change into but judging by the size and quality of them, they belonged to Gabriele.

It was with great reluctance that she slipped a black T-shirt on. It fell to her knees and looked like a sack. Much better.

What wasn't better was the faint trace of cologne permeating through the fabric cleaner. It had to be Gabriele's. It smelt too much like him to belong to anyone else. She hated that it was a scent she found appealing.

As Esmerelda had whisked her underwear away with the rest of her clothes, Elena reluctantly donned the accompanying shorts. They swamped her.

Holding the shorts up to stop them falling down and trying to forget she had Gabriele's scent clinging to her, she set out to find him.

Retracing the route through the cavernous interior, she

found her way to the top deck. She stood at the rail that overlooked the pool deck below, was about to turn back when a figure in the pool made her do a double-take.

Instinct told her it was Gabriele powering his way through the water.

For some incredibly strange reason her heart accelerated, her hold on the rail tightening.

Up and down he swam, his back muscles rippling with the movement. No wonder he had such a fabulous physique...

He reached the end but instead of doing an immediate about-turn and setting off again as he had done thus far, he twisted round and looked up.

Mortified to have been caught...admiring him... Elena went to step back but stopped herself in time. Hiding would only confirm that she'd been spying.

Instead, she held her head high and walked down the wide stairs to the pool deck. By the time she'd reached the bottom Gabriele had hauled himself out of the pool and was rubbing a towel over his face.

Dear Lord...

With the water dripping off his honed bronzed skin and nothing but a pair of tight black swim shorts on with a definite bulge in them...

Feeling her cheeks turn scarlet, Elena hurried to take a seat at a table where a jug of water and a couple of glasses had been laid.

From the corner of her eye she saw him methodically dry himself before slinging the towel over his shoulder and joining her.

He flashed a quick smile and poured them both a drink.

'Do I assume your reappearance means you have come to a decision?' he asked, placing her glass before her.

'Not quite.' She took a drink of the cold water, wiped her mouth with her thumb and took a deep breath. 'There are some things we need to discuss first.'

'Such as?'

'If I agree to marry you, I want a signed agreement that all the so-called evidence you have against my father will be destroyed.'

'The contract being drafted has that specified.'

'You're drafting one already?'

'Yes. It will set out in black and white exactly what this marriage will be so there is no room for doubt on either side.'

'Isn't that rather presumptuous? I haven't said yes.'

'You will,' he said with an arrogant shrug.

She sucked in air through her teeth and willed herself not to bite.

'Your father's liberty depends on it,' he added.

Growing up in an all-male household, Elena was well used to the male ego. Any man stupid enough to think she was inferior because of her gender or size soon learnt the error of his ways. It had delighted her father that his little princess was brainier than her brothers—admittedly not hard—and had never lost a physical fight against any of them either.

In the Ricci household you learnt to take care of yourself from a very young age.

Gabriele's arrogance—different from her brothers' and far more acute—was just another thing to add to the list of things to despise about him.

'Will I be expected to give up my job?'

'No, but I will expect you to make concessions on your workload as I will have to make concessions on mine. For our marriage to be believable we will have to marry our diaries as well as ourselves.'

She eyed him with a suspicious glare. 'And that will be in the contract?'

'Yes. Anything else?'

'Your demand for me to have your child is abhorrent and not something I can agree to.'

'Let me be clear about a couple of things.' Gabriele leaned forward, taking in the whiteness of her face. 'My only reason for marrying you is to hurt your father. You know as well as I do that our marriage will crush him. You carrying a Mantegna child will be the ultimate destruction for his pride.'

'You can't bring a child into a marriage like this,' she said hotly. 'It's immoral.'

'A Ricci lecturing me on morals?' He raised a brow and tutted.

'Why would you even want to have a child with me? You hate me. You could have a baby with anyone.'

'But I don't want *anyone*. I want you.'

Her slim shoulders rose. 'Why?'

'When my father and I were arrested four years ago, I was engaged to be married. I pleaded guilty to save my father's neck but Sophia, my fiancée, chose not to believe that or believe me. She couldn't handle the media scrutiny and the associated shame it brought on her and ended our relationship. Believe me, I will never trust another woman again. After what your father did I will not trust *anyone*. I am the last of my line. You having my child will mean the Mantegna name lives on.'

Merely thinking about Sophia made him feel sick. She'd broken their engagement in a clinical fashion that hadn't left him devastated for the loss of her love but furious that he had ever believed in it. He couldn't believe he'd been ready to commit his life to such a disloyal, spineless creature. Thankfully there had been no time to brood; his over-riding priorities at the time being to stop Mantegna Cars being pulled under and to protect his parents. That he'd only succeeded in the former was something he would live with for the rest of his life.

'And you could love a child with Ricci blood in it?' Elena challenged.

He shrugged. 'The child will be half Mantegna. That will dilute the impact.'

'What a disgusting thing to say.'

'I'm merely being honest. If you agree to this marriage then I don't want there to be any room for misunderstandings. Any child we have would be an innocent in all this and I do not hurt innocents.'

'You're hurting *me*.'

'You're not an innocent.'

She flinched and squeezed her eyes shut but he ignored her distress.

If she was anyone other than Ignazio's daughter and favourite, closest child, he would feel sorry for her.

Then again, if she was anyone else he wouldn't dream of the actions he was taking.

Elena was a special case.

Elena had watched his father be accused of a crime she knew damn well her own father had committed. She had seen Gabriele take the rap, had seen the worldwide media coverage, had likely seen the footage of him entering the federal prison system, and seen, mere days later, the coverage that his father's great heart had given up on him. And through it all, she'd said nothing.

She'd allowed his father to die with his only child imprisoned for a crime her own father had committed and his wife all alone in a country whose language she had never quite mastered. And she'd done nothing.

As far as he was concerned she was as guilty for his father's death as Ignazio, and he wouldn't rest until every single Ricci had paid the price for their heinous lies and betrayal.

If she wanted to know what real pain was she should walk in his shoes for an hour.

'Our marriage will last for as long as it takes to conceive and then we will go our separate ways.'

Her face went even whiter, her horror stark. 'You would take a child away from its mother?'

'I'm not the monster in this relationship,' he said. 'I'd be willing to have joint custody but the condition would be that it has no contact with any member of your family.'

'You *are* a monster,' she spat. 'How you can even think about bringing a child into the world under such conditions...'

'Nevertheless they *are* my conditions. Take it or leave it. I want a child. I want revenge. I can marry those two desires by marrying you. And look on the positives of having my child—as soon as you're pregnant you'll have outlived your usefulness and I will set you free. It is up to you. Or you can take your chances with the law.'

'Let's say for argument's sake that I do agree to have a baby with you.' Desperation laced her husky voice. 'How are you going to have...have...sex with a woman you hate?'

'Are you really that naïve about the workings of a man?' he mocked. 'Our libidos tend to work independently from our brains. You're not a bad-looking woman. I'm sure making a baby with you won't be too much of a hardship.'

If Elena had anything else to say she must have become incapable. Her eyes were wide and full of fury and outrage.

'It is best our cards are laid on the table,' he said. 'And now that you know where you stand on everything, have you come to a decision? Will you marry me?'

Her lips pulled together. He could hear her breathing.

'As long as that contract guarantees you will not take my baby away from me and as long as it guarantees you will destroy the alleged evidence and that you will stop the whispering campaign you've been conducting against my family then yes, I will marry you.'

He allowed himself the satisfaction of a smile.

But Elena wasn't finished.

Hands clenched into balls, she said, 'But you have to

buy me a house in Florence and one close to your home in New York.'

'What on earth for?'

'If we're sharing custody it means I can always be close to our child whenever it's with you and be there if it needs me.'

He was surprised to find she had some latent maternal genes in her.

'And I want it stipulated, in black and white, that you will never bad-mouth me or my family to our child.'

From the look on Elena's face, Gabriele judged this was the deal breaker. He had to admire her. She had spirit. And, despite being a Ricci, compassion for a child who hadn't yet been created.

'Okay,' he agreed with a lazy shrug. 'I can agree to that.'

'I want it written in the contract.'

'Consider it done.'

'Good. But just so you know, you're not the only one who can hold a grudge and wish for vengeance.' She rose from her chair and leaned forward so her furious eyes were mere inches from his. 'When this is over I will personally see that you pay. There will not be a minute of the day when you don't regret what you've done to me. I will see you burn in hell for this.'

Unexpectedly, something cold raced up his spine.

'I'm already in hell,' he said bitterly. 'Your father put me there.'

Her top lip curled. 'Then I will make it my mission in life to keep you there.'

CHAPTER FOUR

THE SOUND OF a helicopter flying overhead made Elena shade her eyes and look to the skies.

She was sitting on the balcony of her cabin, exactly where she'd been for the past two hours since she'd walked away from Gabriele, before she'd given into the temptation to punch him in the face.

Never in her entire life had she hated someone. Never in her entire life had she felt so, so, so...*much* towards another person.

Her early childhood had been spent rallying against the injustice of being the only female in a household of males. She had come to realise the only way to get their respect was to behave like them. She might have been home educated, unlike her brothers who were sent to smart schools, and she might have been sheltered from the outside world, but within the household she had turned her anger to her advantage and become one of the boys. She had forced her brothers' respect and at the same time gained her father's.

Now she felt as helpless and angry as she had at the age of ten when she'd finally comprehended that the education she dreamt of, one where she could be with other girls her age, had been denied her. Even now she still struggled with other women. She just couldn't relate to them. First kisses, first attempts at putting make-up on, everything that went with being a female adolescent had been denied her. She had learned to embrace it.

Well she wouldn't embrace this situation. Gabriele would pay for this. She didn't know how or when or... anything, but she would make him pay.

She couldn't even think about what it would mean to have his child.

A child. A baby. The one thing she'd never thought she would have.

Having intended to spend her life as a Vestal Virgin, Elena had reconciled herself to never having a child of her own. Her brothers had taken too much glee in sharing salacious stories of their conquests. She'd listened to all the sordid details and heard their obvious contempt for the women who were always, without exception, referred to as whores.

By the time she'd turned fifteen Elena had known she would rather stay a virgin than be subjected to that kind of disgusting treatment. She would never allow herself to be treated as a piece of meat. Yes, there were ways to conceive a child that didn't involve getting physical with a man, but they weren't ways she could bring herself to consider.

A knock on the cabin door brought her out of her reverie.

She unlocked it and found Gabriele standing there, a thin document file in one hand, the case she'd taken to Nutmeg Island in the other.

'Where did you get that?' she asked, amazed.

'I had it couriered to my assistant. She brought it on the helicopter.'

'But how?'

'A friendly police officer retrieved it.' He smiled a secret smile. 'Carter's gang disabled the security monitors before you arrived. All your security team saw on their screens was the feed from the day before. No one knows you were on the island and I would imagine the gang won't mention it unless they want to add assault and attempted kidnap to their list of charges.'

Immediately her blood pressure rose. 'So they get away with it?'

'Not at all.' A darkness crossed his features. 'They will pay for it. They were arrested before they could leave the island and can all look forward to a hefty sentence in a prison that will make the one I was incarcerated in look like a holiday camp.'

He threw a thin document file on her bed before she could argue any more about it. 'Here's the contract.'

'You don't waste time.'

'Read through it, sign it and we can leave.'

'Are we at Tampa Bay?' She hadn't seen any sign of land from her balcony.

'No. You've already reached your decision so my helicopter will take us inland to my jet. My assistant and lawyer are waiting in the saloon—they'll act as witnesses for the contract.'

'You can't expect me to sign it now?'

'It's written clearly and concisely. It won't take you more than five minutes to read it.'

Giving him a baleful glare, Elena leaned over the bed to grab the file and see for herself.

As she turned back again, pulling the elegantly bound papers out, something about him made her stop.

There was an expression on his face she'd never seen before. A look in his eyes…

Heat pooled in her stomach and spread through her, climbing up to crawl through the veins in her face.

She'd taken his oversized shorts off the second she'd arrived back in her cabin.

She'd leaned over to grab the file totally forgetting she had no underwear on.

He'd *seen* her.

Gabriele's breathing had become heavy, his eyes containing a blackness that was quite unlike the angry circles of ice he usually looked at her with.

Please, something, anything, swallow her up right now.

He'd *seen* her.

His throat moved and then he coughed and took a step back before pulling a small tube from his pocket. 'This is some lotion for you to put on your wrists—it should help with the bruising.

'I will leave you to dress and read through the contract.' He no longer looked at her, his voice even deeper than normal. 'I will send someone for you in thirty minutes.'

He didn't wait for a response, throwing the tube on the bed and leaving the cabin in three long strides.

Gabriele concentrated hard on the conversation with his lawyer, discussing the finer details of the contract Milo had drafted for him.

Milo knew better than to try and talk Gabriele from the route he was taking. He had been his family's lawyer for over two decades, and there was little about Gabriele that Milo didn't know. It was this familiarity that made him sense the lawyer didn't approve of this particular route.

Whether his lawyer approved was irrelevant. As for Anna Maria, his assistant, she was too well paid to have an opinion on anything.

His lawyer and assistant were the only people to know the truth and he intended to keep it that way. To the rest of the world, especially to Ignazio, his and Elena's marriage would be the real deal.

It was only when Milo and Anna Maria both rose that he knew Elena had arrived.

Straight away his mind flashed to the image he'd been fighting not to see for thirty minutes.

The base of her bottom.

The base of her white, peachy, perfect bottom. The way it darkened at the base of the curve to show the promise of her hidden femininity.

One look and his pulse had paused for a heartbeat then surged into life, heat throbbing through his bloodstream.

He hadn't had such a visceral reaction to a woman since his teenage years. Arranging his features into neutrality, he turned his head to see her standing by his chair. She'd changed into another pair of long, boyish shorts and a plain white T-shirt, her hair now neatly tied back.

Gabriele made the introductions.

She shook hands with them both before casting him with another of the baleful glares he was becoming accustomed to.

He waited until Milo and Anna Maria had left them alone before saying, 'That is not the kind of greeting a man expects from his fiancée when in public.'

'Get used to it.'

He fixed her with a stare. 'I do not expect you take pleasure in my company but when we are in the company of others I expect you to treat me with respect and adoration. That will begin immediately.'

'Adoration?' she snorted, taking the seat opposite him and crossing her legs.

'Have you read through the contract? It details it quite clearly.'

She met his eyes.

Colour flooded her cheeks and he knew that she knew what he had seen.

She snapped her gaze away and cleared her throat. 'As long as you only expect adoration in public. In private you can sing for it.'

'I wouldn't expect anything else,' he replied sardonically. 'Do you have any questions about the contract?'

'The sleeping arrangements...'

'Are non-negotiable,' he supplied before she could go any further. 'For as long as our marriage lasts, it will be a traditional marriage, one in which we make a child.'

'We can use insemination.' Elena knew she sounded desperate but she didn't care. How could she sleep with him? He might be a walking pack of gorgeous testosterone but she *hated* him.

He laughed. For once it sounded genuine. 'No. We will make a baby in the traditional way. The world will believe our marriage is for real. Given the history between our families, our marriage will generate media scrutiny like nothing you will have ever experienced. Our staff will be besieged and offered money which would tempt even the saintliest person. We sleep together and that's the end of the matter.'

Elena squeezed her eyes closed and wished herself away from this nightmare she had fallen into.

The contract had been as concise as Gabriele had promised but seeing the terms written so bluntly made her wish there had been some superfluous words to take the edge off.

Divorce proceedings shall be initiated by Party 2, Elena Ricci, only when conception has been achieved and subject to that Party 1, Gabriele Mantegna, shall initiate divorce proceedings without any encumbrances.

There were even long clauses regarding the custody of their mythical child, clauses that, while splitting custody evenly, gave Gabriele all rights with regards to education and *'moral upbringing'* whatever that meant. He'd included her demands but had also stipulated his stance that her family must not be allowed any contact with their child or else all custody rights would be revoked and he would become sole guardian.

That he would use an innocent child as a pawn in his game of vengeance made her blood fire with fury. What kind of despicable monster would do such a thing?

Yet a different kind of heat suffused her as she imagined sharing a bed with him.

She'd never shared a bed with anyone in her life. To think of sharing one with a man as overtly masculine as Gabriele, of being burrowed under the same sheets…

'The evidence against my father. I want it destroyed now, not when we divorce.'

He shook his head. 'If I destroy it now there will be nothing to stop you from backing out of our deal.'

'Isn't my word good enough?'

'You're a Ricci. Your word is as useful as a chocolate teapot.'

A choked laugh razed her throat and she coughed.

One day she would learn not to laugh at inappropriate moments. Unfortunately it wasn't something she had any control over and completely involuntary.

Finally daring to look at him, she found his quizzical gaze upon her.

'You're amused?' he asked with an arched eyebrow.

'I have a warped funny bone.'

A glimmer of light flashed in his eyes but it vanished as quickly as it came.

'Do you have any other issues with the contract?' he said.

'Other than the entire document itself?'

'Anything specific,' he clarified drily.

'I have issues with everything but no, not anything specific.'

'Excellent. Then let's get it signed and we can start our new life together.'

The helicopter took them straight to the airport where Gabriele's flight crew were waiting for them in his private jet. Before long they were in the air and on their way to New York.

'Why New York?' she asked. She'd assumed they would go straight to his home in Italy, what with them both being Italian.

'Because we can marry in a couple of days there.'

'That soon?'

'We'll get the paperwork sorted on Monday and marry on Tuesday.'

She swallowed.

Everything was moving so quickly it felt as if she'd filled up on rocket fuel.

'After we've married we'll go to Florence. I'm launching a new car at my headquarters there in a month's time so I need to be on site.'

'I thought Mantegna Cars were based in the US?' Despite herself, her curiosity was piqued. As a child she'd loved it when her father had taken her out for a drive in one of his new Mantegna Cars. They'd always been so glamorous and powerful, ahead of their time in the gadget department. She'd always been proud that so many of those gadgets had come from her father's factories.

'Florence is Mantegna Car's birthplace and it's always been our European headquarters.' There was a hardness in his face. 'My parents loved their time in America but with retirement around the corner, they wanted to go home. As you know, my father died before he could make it back. Being incarcerated solidified the decision for me. Florence is my main home now, and it's back to being the headquarters of our entire company.'

A gleam came into his eyes, dispelling the hardness. 'Just think, come the launch, you might have the seed of life growing inside you.'

'But the nightmare won't be over, will it?' She crossed her legs as an unexpected ripple of heat pulsed low in her. 'A child will tie me to you for the rest of my life.'

'As long as you keep to the contractual obligations you signed, there will be minimal contact between us when we part.'

'Zero contact would be preferable.'

Ignoring his low, mocking laughter, Elena clamped her lips together and turned her head to look out of the window, staring at the pillowy clouds beneath them.

To her chagrin, when she next looked at him, Gabriele had fallen asleep.

She was surprised his conscience allowed him to sleep.

But then, she supposed one must have a conscience in the first place, which he absolutely did not.

She ran her hand over her face then tilted her chair back and curled into it, breathing deeply to quell the rising nausea in her belly.

She could go and have a sleep in the bedroom as Gabriele had offered when they'd boarded but she wasn't yet prepared to get under the covers of any bed belonging to him. Not voluntarily. Not until she had to.

With the cabin crew undertaking their duties quietly, bringing her a fresh supply of coffee and a plate of delicious sandwiches, the most her ragged stomach could handle, she couldn't stop her gaze flitting to the sleeping form opposite her.

It was the first time she'd really had the chance to study him unobserved.

They said the devil took beguiling forms to trap people. In Gabriele's case this was true. He really was handsome. Sinfully handsome.

Sleeping, arms crossed loosely over his chest, his head tilted to the right, his dark hair touching his shoulder, his top lip covering the bottom, he looked as if he should be in a Caravaggio picture; a chiselled, handsome man emerging from an impenetrable darkness that not only surrounded him but lived within him.

Gabriele stepped into the penthouse apartment he'd bought a year ago on his release from prison. Spacious—for Manhattan proportions—and full of light, it was the perfect antidote to the cramped cell he'd slept in for two years. He considered himself lucky that Milo and his legal team had managed to get him into the minimum security camp and that his roommate had been an elderly 'white collar' criminal. Like himself.

But it had still been a prison. He'd still been locked away, his liberty taken from him.

Elena followed him inside, through the galley and into the living room, her head turning in all directions. She stood at the walled window that overlooked Central Park. 'This must have cost you a fortune.'

'It did.' Manhattan prices were extortionate by anyone's standards. Of all his properties this had cost him the most. He would pay it tenfold. New York had an energy to it he'd never found anywhere else, and here he was only an hour from his mother.

'Come, I'll show you around.'

With obvious reluctance, she stepped away from the window and followed him back into the galley.

'Kitchen,' he said, throwing open the door on the other side of the elevator. 'My housekeepers have the weekend off so you'll be able to settle in with privacy, but this is normally Michael and Lisa's domain. That room through there is their staff room.'

'You cook?' she asked.

'Badly. You?'

'Badly.'

Their eyes met and for a moment he was certain her lips were trying to smile.

'I've made reservations at Ramones for us, so we won't starve in their absence.'

'We're eating out tonight?'

'The sooner we're seen in public, the better. Ramones is the perfect place—there's always a paparazzo camped there.'

'I should call my father.'

'Call him tomorrow.'

'I don't want him to see the pictures before I've told him about…us.'

'You decided to take a last-minute trip to New York. We bumped into each other and decided to go for a meal to bury the hatchet,' he said, reminding her of the agreed script they had come to after signing the contract. 'You can tell him this tomorrow.'

'I can't believe I'm going to lie to my own father.'

'This has to be believable, Elena. Any hint that what we have isn't real then the deal is off and I take the evidence to the FBI.'

He led her out of the kitchen and back into the galley, ignoring the laser burn of her glare in his back.

'Guest room, guest room, guest room...our room.' He stepped inside and opened a door. 'En suite.' He opened another. 'My dressing room.' And another. 'Your dressing room.'

Elena peered inside and nodded, but didn't say anything.

'I'm going to take a shower. All the guest rooms have their own en suites if you want to freshen up. I'm afraid when I bought this property it wasn't with a future wife in mind or I would have had adjoining en suites put in. Can you be ready to leave in a couple of hours?'

She nodded curtly.

'Good. If you need anything, let me know.'

Her green eyes met his. 'The only thing I need is for you to admit you were wrong about me and wrong about my father and let me go.'

'You were right—you do have a warped sense of humour.'

Elena got ready in the guest room the furthest from the master suite, trying not to imagine that Gabriele was, at that very moment, naked in the shower.

Surely, any minute now, she would awake on her Oslo office sofa and find the past couple of days had been nothing but a bad dream.

She'd been tied up and threatened with kidnapping and, worse, rescued by the man who hated her entire family. She'd been forced to sign a contract for a marriage that would save her father from prison but would result in a baby, and been installed in a luxury Manhattan apartment. All in twenty-four hours.

Who knew what tomorrow would bring? Maybe she would wake up on the moon.

She was ready before Gabriele and took the opportunity to explore his apartment further.

Having grown up with wealth, she wasn't fazed by its opulence but had to admit he had exquisite taste. The high ceilings and floor-to-ceiling windows cried out for majestic furniture to match and he had stepped up to the mark. White walls, thick cream carpets her toes sank into and plush soft brown leather sofas that managed to be exquisite and comfortable all at the same time...it was like being in a homely art gallery with some very surreal paintings.

One particular framed painting caught her eye, a portrait of a man whose features were, upon closer inspection, painted entirely with fruits and vegetables; a pear for a nose, mange tout for the upper eyelids...and was that a husk of corn used as an ear...?

'Do you like it?'

So absorbed had she been in the painting that she hadn't heard Gabriele enter the room.

'It's brilliant. Is it a Giuseppe Arcimboldo?'

'You recognise it?' There was an approving tone in his voice.

She nodded. 'I love his work. It's mad and witty and so clever. I could look at it for hours.'

'This is only a reproduction but my home in Florence has a couple of his original pieces.'

A tiny shiver traced up her spine at the mention of Florence. Italy was her home. It was where Gabriele was from. Their respective families' lives had been turned into a soap opera there and she dreaded the reception that news of their marriage would bring in their home country.

'Are you going to change?' he asked. 'We need to leave soon.'

'I *have* changed.'

'You're not intending to go out like that?' The approval had gone.

Turning her gaze from the painting, she looked at him and saw disbelief on his face.

'What's wrong with it?' Having only packed for the weekend, she'd opted for the clothes she'd intended to travel back to Europe in: a navy-blue trouser suit with a high-necked white blouse and a pair of flat black shoes.

'You look like you're going to a business meeting. Have you anything else to wear? Anything remotely feminine?'

Bristling, she scowled. 'This is what I feel comfortable in. All my clothes are the same—trouser suits.'

'And when you're not working?'

She shrugged. 'Clothes don't interest me.'

'They do now,' he stated grimly. 'Stand still a minute.'

Burning under the weight of his scrutiny, she nonetheless held her head high, wondering what the big deal was. Clothes were clothes. They were worn to protect you from the elements and, in a business environment, to convey a professional approach. Everything else was superfluous.

'Untuck your blouse,' he ordered.

She did as he said, wondering what he was thinking.

'Now tie it into a knot around your waist.'

At her puzzled look, he sighed and reached for the base of her blouse, undoing the bottom two buttons.

'What are you doing?' she demanded, stepping back, unnerved.

'Unsmartening you. Now tie it into a knot and undo the top three buttons—unless you want me to do it for you?'

'Touch me again and I'll punch you in the nose.'

He raised his eyebrows but his tone remained civil. 'We're going out in public in a few minutes. You have to be comfortable with my touch if we're going to convince your father and the world that we've fallen madly in love.'

'I doubt a decade of marriage would make me comfortable with a man who wants to destroy my family.' And he absolutely could destroy them. It was the only reason she stood there taking this humiliation.

'Fake it.'

As he was looming so threateningly over her, she quickly did as he bid. Feeling like a complete fool, she unbuttoned her blouse. 'Anything else you want me to do? Get a face transplant?'

'You could do with a damn good haircut but seeing as we don't have time for that either tie it into a knot or wear it down. Ponytails are for schoolgirls. And tug your trousers down so they sit on your hips and not around your belly button.'

When she was done and had retied her hair into his requested knot, she put her hands on her hips. 'Am I presentable now?'

'Roll your trousers up a couple of inches.'

If she glared at him any more there was a good chance the wind would change direction and her face would stay that way.

Crouching down, she rolled her trousers up so they hung above her ankles.

'Have you any other shoes?' he asked when she was upright again.

'I have a pair of running shoes.'

He pulled a face. 'Then you will have to do as you are but first thing in the morning, we're going clothes shopping.'

'You do not get to choose my wardrobe.'

'I wouldn't think it necessary if you didn't have such dire taste. You dress like a straitjacketed man.'

'I do not.'

'You don't dress like a woman. Personally I couldn't care less what you wear,' he continued, speaking over her indignant yelp of protest, 'but the fact is you're supposed to be a woman in love. Women in love take pride in their appearance and the clothes they wear.'

'Do they?'

'They do.' A look of suspicion crossed his features. When he next spoke, it was with a hint of hesitation. 'You *have* been in a relationship before?'

'I'm twenty-five,' she scoffed, evading the question, damned if she was going to admit she hadn't even been on a date before. It was none of his business.

Even if she had been so inclined, there hadn't been any chance of boyfriends growing up, what with a solo education and three ready-made chaperones in the form of her brothers. By the time she was old enough to ditch the chaperones, she'd sworn off men for life. She knew everything there was to know about them and how they and their friends treated the women in their lives and spoke behind their backs. They were pigs. All men were.

Maybe she was being unkind to pigs.

'If I don't feel comfortable in what I'm wearing it will be harder for me to pretend to be in love,' she pointed out.

She was glad she'd thought of her brothers and the idiots they called friends. If she pretended Gabriele was one of them she could handle him without any problem whatsoever. *They* didn't unnerve her or threaten to overwhelm her with their latent masculinity as Gabriele did.

'You can choose your clothes but you *will* burn your existing wardrobe.'

'I'll put it in storage for the day we go our separate ways.'

'You know what you'll have to do to make that day come closer.'

More colour crept over her face but she didn't drop her gaze. 'Or maybe you'll get so sick of living with me that *you* end it before a baby's conceived.'

He shrugged a hefty shoulder and leaned forward, his eyes drilling into her. 'I spent two years in prison for a crime I didn't commit. In that time my father died and my mother's health deteriorated. Every day we spend together is another day of purgatory for your father. I have no time limit.'

For the first time a whisper of doubt blew at her.

Could he be telling the truth?

She discounted it as soon as she thought it. Her brothers might be pigs but her father was nothing like them. Her father would never have set Alfredo up. They'd been lifelong *friends*.

All the same, an unsettled feeling lay in her as they left the apartment a short while later, quite unlike the nausea she felt at the deal she was striking with the devil himself.

CHAPTER FIVE

RAMONES WAS A tiny restaurant in Times Square, bursting to the brim with diners. As Gabriele had promised, the paparazzi were stationed outside.

Once inside, Elena understood why.

'Is that Gary Milwake?' she whispered as they were led past a couple chatting happily in a booth by the window.

'It is,' he confirmed. 'And that's Serafina de Angelo with him.'

Gary Milwake was the breakthrough movie star of the year, his dining partner the star of the biggest-selling box set of the decade.

'They're waving at you.' She tried not to screech.

'That's because Gary's an acquaintance. He drove a Mantegna supercar in *The Long Drive By*. I took him for his original test drive.'

She took her seat, trying in vain not to look too excited at all the other familiar faces. While Gabriele ordered a bottle of wine for them, she couldn't stop herself staring. There was a pop star dining with a man who she didn't recognise but was definitely not the man she was reported to be dating, and she said as much.

'Eating here guarantees publicity,' Gabriele said, opening his menu. 'Tomorrow the Internet will be abuzz with gossip about her. That's all that matters—publicity.'

She wrinkled her nose. 'How sordid.'

He shrugged. 'It's business for them. Column inches matter. Now stop staring at everyone and look adoringly at me.'

'If this is our first date then I wouldn't look at you adoringly,' she contradicted, speaking off the top of her head.

Never mind looking at him with adoration, every time she looked at him she felt a snake uncoil itself within her and want to launch at him. 'This is the evening we play "getting to know you".'

'A fair point. However, even on a first date people who are attracted to each other lean in closely together and speak intimately. They do not spend their time star spotting.'

She smiled and tried fluttering her eyelashes. 'I've never met a star before.'

'Your family has always mingled with celebrities. And you look like you have something in your eye.'

'I'm trying to look adoring.'

'Just lean towards me and remember, whatever you say, say it with a smile on your face.'

She rested her arms on the table and leaned closer to the face she found more handsome every time she looked. Smiling brightly, she said, 'Is that better, you savage bastard?'

Mimicking her actions and with a full-wattage beam, he replied, 'It's a start, you poisonous viper.'

'Is that the best you can do? My brothers have much better derogatory names for me than that.'

'They've had many more years of practice. Look at *me*,' he added when her attention was taken by another passing film star.

'Sorry.'

'How can you be so star struck when your family have partied with celebrities for years?'

'My father and my brothers have. You forget, I run the European division. I have nothing to do with what happens in the US and the rest of the world.'

'By choice?'

'I started off working in Rome then gradually progressed to take over Italy, then the rest of Europe.'

'Nepotism at its finest.'

'That's rich coming from a man who took the same route through *his* family firm.'

'The difference is I've enhanced what we already had. When I joined Mantegna Cars we had a turnover of half a billion dollars. Within five years of me joining that figure had tripled because of the diversifications I put in to trade on our name.'

Her smile dropped a fraction as she tried to think of what she'd personally done to enhance her division and boost Ricci Components' profits. Nothing sprang to mind.

'Now we are one of the top car manufacturers in the world,' he continued, 'even with the battering we took at the hands of your father's fraud and lies.'

She couldn't stop the glare from forming and had to fight hard to paste another smile on her face.

Thankfully, the waiter returned with their wine. After a glass had been poured for them both and they'd given their food orders, Gabriele raised his glass to her.

'To the start of a wonderful new relationship and to the best of nepotism.'

She chinked hers to it and smiled as she said, 'And here's to revenge, which everyone knows is best served cold.'

'I prefer my revenge to be scalding hot but cold serves my needs equally well.'

With mutual antipathy, they both sipped their drinks, both smiling, both firing ice and loathing from their eyes.

As a way to toast their new relationship, Elena thought it very apt.

Gabriele surprised himself by enjoying their meal out. There had been more than a few occasions when he had laughed out loud at the barbs coming from Elena's tongue, all of them dressed with a sweet smile.

Now they were back at his apartment and the slight relaxing of her demeanour in the restaurant might never have been. Elena was back to being as tight as a coiled spring. She'd even stopped throwing barbs at him.

As soon as they'd left the car, thanked his driver, and taken the lift to his apartment and were alone for the first time since leaving, she'd turned to him.

'I'm not sharing a bed with you tonight. The contract stated we share a bed and...' her cheeks turned scarlet but she carried on regardless '...and, do what needs to be done when we're married. We're not married yet. Your housekeepers have the weekend off so there is no one for us to convince of our blossoming romance.'

'They will know if a guest bed has been slept in.'

'I don't care. Not everyone jumps into bed on a first date. They'll assume one of us has some morals.'

He arched a brow. 'Meaning?'

'Meaning they work for *you* so it's doubtful they associate morals with you or the people you call friends. You're a convicted criminal, remember?'

'Are you deliberately trying to anger me?' he asked slowly, holding onto his temper by a whisker.

'What, by speaking the truth? Oh, sorry, I forgot, you believe *my father* to be the criminal.'

Gabriele silently counted to ten, breathing heavily as he did so, staring at this woman who dared speak to him of morals when she came from a family of conscience-less snakes.

She didn't drop her stare, holding her ground with a raised chin and a pursed mouth.

Only her eyes showed vulnerability. It was there, ringing out from them, mingled with the defiance and it tempered the fury that had shot through him.

There was no room in this relationship for pity but as much as he didn't want to put himself in her shoes he could understand why she would feel vulnerable.

'Tonight you can sleep in a guest room,' he agreed, rolling his neck to loosen the knots that had formed in it. 'It's been a long day for both of us. But from tomorrow you sleep with me.'

'There will be no *sex…*' she spat the word as if it were an oath '…until we're married.'

He gave a slow, deliberate smile. 'Which is only three days away. Three days until you're Mrs Mantegna and welcome me into the warmth of your delightful body with open arms.'

'Welcoming? I think not.'

'You expect me to believe that when I've seen the way you undress me with your eyes? Admit it, there's an attraction between us. Inexplicable, I admit, but there all the same.'

Her cheeks flamed with colour, letting him know he'd scored a direct hit.

When he'd made the demand that she have his baby it had been a logical progression to his thoughts on marrying her. He wanted a child but he didn't want the commitment to a woman that went with it. To his mind, Elena having his child was the perfect solution. It would make his revenge on her father almost complete—until he found the evidence to clear his name it would *never* be complete— and give him the heir he so wanted.

She was dressed in the most hideous outfit he'd ever seen on a woman, even with the improvements he'd made to it. But still his imagination ran amok wondering what lay beneath; the image of her naked bottom never far from his thoughts. All that, and the way she fought fire with fire… it all conspired to make his loins tighten in a way he'd almost forgotten.

Elena Ricci was the complete reverse of what he usually found attractive in a woman but there was something about her his senses responded to.

She stared at him, her eyes flashing, but then gave a slow, deliberate smile of her own. 'The only thing I will welcome is the blow to your ego every time you remember that you could only have me by blackmail.'

'Then I will be sure to take extra special enjoyment every time I make you come.'

Colour heightened not only her face but her neck too.

'You're crude and you are not a gentleman.' Turning on her heel, she marched from the living room, saying over her shoulder, 'I'm going to bed. Goodnight. Hope the bed-bugs bite.'

'Elena,' he called after her.

'What?'

'Next time you try and rouse my anger to keep me out of your bed, know your efforts will be wasted. Any more excuses and I rip our contract up and throw your entire family to the wolves.'

She left the living room without looking back.

Elena awoke early after a night of fitful sleep, rising shortly after the sun.

With nothing but a pair of pyjamas on, she padded to the kitchen in search of coffee only to find Gabriele had beaten her to it, already showered, shaved and dressed. He'd even been out and bought bagels for them both.

'Bagels, for breakfast?' she mumbled, shuffling onto a chair at the kitchen table, feeling awkward with her sleep-crumpled face and mussed hair.

'You don't visit New York often?'

She shook her head and opened the box hers was in. 'This is only my second time here.'

He stared at her, making her feel even more self-conscious. When he looked at her like that it felt as if he were trying to pry open her thoughts.

No one had ever looked at her like that before.

After a long bout of silence broken only by her nibbling as quietly as she could at the bacon and cream cheese bagel, which turned out to be delicious, she excused herself to take a shower.

'We'll make a move when you're ready,' he said to her retreating figure. 'We're going to get you a new wardrobe and have you made over. I've booked you in with a stylist.'

'You're not going to police my purchases?'

'No. Your stylist will guide you in selecting clothes you feel comfortable in. I'm going to the office.'

'It's Sunday.' Even she, a self-admitted workaholic, didn't go to the office on a Sunday. That didn't mean she didn't work on the supposed day of rest, only that she didn't expect anyone else to.

'We've a busy time coming up,' he answered with a shrug. 'There's some stuff I need to get done before we head off to Florence and I won't have many opportunities after today.'

Two hours later, they entered an exclusive store on Fifth Avenue.

Having had such a rubbish night's sleep, Elena was well aware of how drained she looked. Even her hair, thin as it was at the best of times, was lank.

When the stylist, a tall, immaculately dressed woman in her forties, strode towards her with an outstretched hand, she felt even more conspicuous.

Gabriele greeted her as if she were an old friend, kissing her on each cheek.

'I will leave you in Liana's capable hands, *tesoro*,' he said to Elena, his tone affectionate.

Had he brought other women here?

The strange pang that twisted her stomach was smothered when he caught her off guard, wrapping his arms around her and placing a brief kiss to her lips.

The briefest of kisses. Tiny. Insubstantial. And yet enough to set her heart fluttering.

He pulled away, rubbing her arms for good measure.

'My phone will be on if you need me, otherwise, if I don't hear from you I'll pick you up at four.'

Too shell-shocked by the unexpected heat of his mouth on hers and his fruity, masculine scent playing in her senses to respond with anything but a weak, 'Okay,' she watched him stroll out, her eyes drifting to the tight buttocks wrapped in a pair of snug-fitting black jeans, which also emphasised the length and muscularity of his thighs.

She dug the nail of her middle finger into the flesh of her thumb.

That was what happened when you didn't get a good night's sleep. Your body reacted in unpredictable ways when the monster you were being forced to marry kissed you.

It was only because she hadn't been prepared for it. Next time she would be, and would bite his lip for good measure.

Liana bore her off to an elevator, asking questions about her taste in music and books and films that sounded innocuous but which Elena was certain had meaning. The stylist was trying to figure her out.

Before they'd reached the floor they were heading to, she could hold it back no longer. 'Have you dressed many of Gabriele's lady friends?'

'He brought his mother here at Christmas.' Liana used such a sympathetic tone that a ripple of unease ran through her, making Elena wonder what it was about Gabriele's mother that elicited such a tone.

When they reached the intended floor, Liana knew exactly where she wanted to take her.

Following in her wake, she passed two women, one of whom was holding a small baby.

She turned back for a second look, her heart thundering.

She was going to have one. She was going to have a baby.

The one thing she had never allowed herself to dream of having.

But to get one she would have to have sex with Gabriele. God help her.

And God help her that a thrill of heat pooled in her abdomen every time she imagined it.

Liana whisked her into a private dressing room and brought armfuls of clothes in a steady stream, from elegant business outfits to cocktail dresses, to everything in between.

Although reluctant to try them on, feeling that to do so would in itself be a victory for Gabriele, to her surprise Elena soon found she was enjoying herself. Even more surprisingly, the clothes Liana selected were items she would have chosen for herself if she'd ever given it more than a few seconds' thought. Nothing too girly, which she would have rejected on the spot, yet definitely feminine.

The only time she truly wanted to put her foot down was when Liana measured her bra size and brought in sexy little items of lingerie. She could hardly say, 'No thank you, it would be a waste as I couldn't care less what Gabriele thinks of my underwear,' because that hardly fitted the image of a woman newly in love. Elena did manage to dissuade the stylist from checking the fit of them for herself, which she considered to be a personal victory.

Left alone with a pile of bras, she gazed at her reflection in the three full-length mirrors. And gazed again.

She looked different. And all she'd done was try on some clothes.

Peering closer, she studied her face, certain something had changed.

Her skin appeared to glow. Her eyes seemed brighter, the green more vivid. Her lips looked fuller.

It had to be the lighting, she told herself, slipping one of the bras on. The owners must have done it to enhance their customers' reflections.

But even her breasts looked fuller, the lacy bra pushing them up and giving her an actual cleavage. Giving her shape.

She couldn't help her mind from flitting, as it had done seemingly every minute since they'd made their agreement, to being in bed with Gabriele.

The thought *terrified* her.

It should repulse her too. After everything he was doing, everything he was demanding, the thought of sharing a bed with him should have her crammed full of revulsion.

The butterflies in her belly shouldn't feel like the flutters of excitement.

An image drifted into her mind of Gabriele peeling the bra from her body…

She shouldn't have these thoughts. Not of him.

When she gave him her body it would be with the minimum of interaction on her part. She would do what she had to do and nothing more. She would not enjoy it.

Her phone went off, a distraction she welcomed until she clicked on the link Gabriele had emailed to her.

A picture of them outside Ramones had been published online. Elena had been dubbed 'The Convicted Italian Stallion's Mystery Date'.

The first seeds of them as a couple had been planted.

Her identity would be revealed sooner rather than later. Her profile in America was non-existent but all it would take was one Italian to read the article and the world would know who she was.

She'd have to phone her dad as soon as they got back to Gabriele's apartment, a thought that made her already tender stomach lurch some more.

There was no time to worry about it though, as it was time for her makeover. Liana gently persuaded her to change into one of her new outfits rather than slip back into her boyish shorts and T-shirt.

In the beauty department she was taken into a private room. There, a flamboyant man named Adrian, who had the most perfectly plucked eyebrows, sat her onto a high stool and studied her face.

'Your eyes!' he exclaimed. 'They are to die for. And your lips…are they natural?'

At her puzzled expression he said, 'No fillers?'

'No.'

'No work at all?'

'No.'

He sighed. 'A natural beauty. Your face is a blank canvas for me to enhance. But first…' He lifted the lank strands of her hair. 'First we do something to this.'

For the next hour her hair was washed, snipped and dried by yet another stylist, all the while Adrian and Liana chatted to her and plied her with coffee. They refused to let her see the end result, Adrian explaining that they 'wanted her to see the whole effect in one go'.

As he got to work on her face, he gently gave details of what he was doing so she could replicate it for herself.

When he was done, he took her hand and helped her down, then led her to a floor-length mirror so she could see the final results.

'What do you think?' he asked, smiling widely.

As she gazed at her reflection, a lump formed in her throat.

It was her but…not.

Her hair had never looked so voluminous. The severe fringe she chopped herself when it got too long had been feathered. Layers had been cut into the length, which still fell across her shoulders, but instead of just hanging there now became a frame for a face that belonged to her but one she had never seen before.

Far from making her look like a clown as she had feared, Adrian's makeover was surprisingly understated.

Her eyes, darkened around the rims, gleamed, the black mascara making them appear rounder. Her cheeks had a subtle hint of blush on them, defining her bone structure.

Peach lipstick had been applied that made her naturally full lips look even plumper.

It was hard to believe...

'Is that really me?' she whispered, her eyes filling. She'd never imagined she could look so feminine. She'd never imagined she could *feel* so feminine. Not her, the little tomboy.

Adrian put an arm around her and hugged her to him. 'Don't cry. If you don't like it we can take it off and try another—'

'No,' she cut him off with a choked laugh. 'I *do* like it. I love it. You're a miracle worker. All of you.'

He shook his head. 'Elena, you are exquisite. Now promise me one thing.'

'If I can.'

'Always use blush.'

Laughing, she threw her arms around him. 'Thank you.'

Bags of cosmetics and face creams had been packaged for her, along with her new wardrobe of clothes. Her shopping trip was over and it was time to pay the bill.

Elena got her credit card out.

Liana shook her head. 'Mr Mantegna has made arrangements to pay.'

About to protest—after all, she was an independent woman, no matter what charge of nepotism Gabriele laid at her door—she had a nice vision of Gabriele receiving the bill. *He* was the one who insisted she get remodelled. *He* could foot it.

And speaking of *he*...

Now it was time to face him.

The heels of the ankle boots she wore gave her a lift in more sense than one. Never mind being two inches taller, she found she held herself taller too as she strode through the main beauty floor with Liana at her side. She didn't know if she was imagining it but she could feel eyes upon her and had to force herself not to stare at the floor in embarrassment. People *never* looked twice at her.

'One more thing,' Liana said suddenly, coming to a halt by the sunglasses section. She considered them for a while before going behind the counter and handing Elena a Cartier box. 'For when you have to deal with the paparazzi,' she said with a knowing smile.

Elena thanked her and put the box in one of the bags containing the cosmetics she was already looking forward to experimenting with.

As much as she told herself that she couldn't care less what Gabriele thought of her makeover, her heart galloped when Liana opened the door to the private waiting room and Gabriele looked up from the laptop he was working on.

His brown-black eyes widened, and he half rose, the laptop almost falling onto the floor in the process.

After six hours in the department store, Gabriele had been prepared for Elena to come out looking better than she had before. After all, she could hardly present herself any worse. He would have had to be blind not to see her innate prettiness, even though she clearly couldn't be bothered to do anything with it, but nothing could have prepared him for the beauty that walked into the room.

Dio, it was like one of those before and after television programmes his mother had liked to watch.

A pair of tight pale blue jeans that came halfway up her calves was topped with a long shimmering silver off-the-shoulder top under which were the straps of a purple bra. The clothes themselves were nothing to shout about but put together with clever plum costume jewellery, black ankle boots and a haircut that screamed *just got out of bed* without having actually just got out of bed…

It was still Elena the tomboy, but with a very sexy, feminine difference.

The pretty shell had been burst open and the intrinsic beauty had emerged.

This was the sexy, beautiful woman he would be marrying in two days.

Aware of Elena and Liana both waiting expectantly for his reaction, he closed his laptop and got to his feet.

'*Tesoro*, you look wonderful,' he said. 'Did you have a good day?'

'Lovely thank you,' she replied with a sweet smile that didn't fool him for a second.

'You deserve it, you work so hard.'

After satisfying himself that all her purchases were being sent to his apartment, Gabriele led Elena out of the store and to his waiting car at the back.

Once they were settled and the driver was making his way through the heavy Manhattan traffic, Gabriele twisted round to look again at Elena.

The unexpected but very welcome news he'd received that afternoon that a senior member of Ignazio's closest team could possibly be bought now took second place to the woman beside him.

Her cheeks were flushed, her eyes bright and there was an air about her he couldn't put his finger on.

'You did enjoy it,' he stated shrewdly. Now they were alone they could go back to being honest with each other.

'Yes,' she admitted. 'I hadn't realised shopping could be fun.'

'How do you normally buy clothes?'

'I dive in and out of the shop and hope whatever I've chosen fits.'

'You're the only daughter from a family with three sons. Why weren't you dressed as a princess?'

She shrugged. 'I always wanted to be a boy like my brothers. I hated that being a girl made me different.'

'Why did it make you different?'

She pulled a face that conveyed she thought he was an idiot for asking.

'I don't have siblings,' he reminded her. 'All my cousins

are boys. Those kind of family dynamics are not something
I've experienced.'

'Girls are considered more delicate than boys. Weaker.
More prone to tears.'

He considered this. 'I think the tears thing is true…'

She sucked in an outraged breath.

'But as for being more delicate, that's bull,' he finished.
'Women *are* different from men, that's a biological fact
but the kind of delicacy you're talking about doesn't exist.'

'I know that. I've spent my entire life proving it.'

'How? By acting like a man?'

'How else could I be taken seriously?' she demanded.
'The only way I was able to gain my brothers' respect was
by being one of the boys.'

'So it wasn't through choice?'

'I *wanted* to be like them. I didn't know how to be a girl
and had no interest in learning.'

'Do you think it would have made any difference if your
mother had lived and been there to guide you?'

Her eyes met his. 'I wouldn't know. I don't remember
her.'

'That's a real shame,' he eventually replied, remembering the Swedish woman who'd always had a ready smile
on her face and a batch of meatballs on the go. Elena could
only have been two when she died. 'She was a nice woman.'

Her brows drew together. 'You knew her?'

'Of course. Our families were friends. Our mothers were
very close.'

'I didn't know that.' A burst of fire sparked in her eyes
and she leaned towards him fiercely. 'If they were such
good friends I would imagine your mother will be very
disappointed with you when she learns that you're forcing
me to marry you.'

'We will never know. She has dementia. My father's
death accelerated the process. There are days she doesn't

even know who I am.' Something else he absolutely blamed her father for and, by extension, Elena herself.

Her latent beauty might now have pushed to the surface but that was all it was: surface.

Beneath the skin she was a Ricci to her core and he would never allow himself to forget it.

CHAPTER SIX

ELENA WAS MIGHTILY relieved to go straight to her father's voicemail.

'Hi, Papà, it's me. I'm in New York, finally taking that holiday you keep nagging me about.' She injected a false laugh, meeting Gabriele's eye.

He was watching her from the dining room table, his expression inscrutable.

'You'll never believe who I bumped into last night— Alfredo Mantegna's son.' She cleared her throat before ploughing on. 'I've decided to stay in New York for the week and do some sightseeing. Christie will be running things for me. Hope you're well. *Ciao.*'

Done, she disconnected the call, then, for good measure, turned the phone off and stuffed it in her favourite of the designer handbags Liana had selected for her, then faced him with her chin up.

'Well? Was that convincing enough?'

'On a scale of one to ten I'd give it a five,' he drawled, rising to his feet. 'Let's see how you perform this evening—see if we can get it to an eight.'

Tonight they were going to dine at another paparazzi-encamped restaurant, a thought that thrilled her as much as swimming in a shark-infested pool. Since their return from shopping, she'd checked the Internet a dozen times to see if her name was out there but so far, nothing.

Throwing him a brittle smile, which more than spoke the caustic response she wanted to give, Elena slung her handbag over her shoulder and headed to the elevator.

Inside, she surreptitiously checked her appearance.

She was pleased to see the magic Adrian had done to her

face was mostly still intact. Scared of damaging his work, all she'd done for their evening out was apply some more of the lipstick she had taken the lid off a dozen times to smell—who knew cosmetics smelt so good?—and spritzed some perfume onto her neck and wrists. She'd changed out of the jeans into a pair of bright red straight-legged trousers and a pair of silver sandals with a low pointy heel, but had opted to keep on the shimmering top she loved so much.

Gabriele's only remark had been to say, 'That is a definite improvement on last night.'

Except the look in his eyes had said something else.

For the first time she wished she had some experience with men, something that would allow her to translate Gabriele's unspoken expressions. All she had was gut instinct but that was becoming unreliable. All she felt when he looked at her was a feeling she couldn't quite interpret but which she was terrified meant nothing but trouble.

Her response had been a glare and a, 'I'm delighted I meet your approval.'

She didn't believe for a second that he was attracted to her.

All Gabriele wanted was what she could give him. He wanted her body. Not her core. Not her soul. He wanted Ignazio's daughter. If she'd had sisters, any of them would have served his purpose equally well.

Now, catching his eye in the mirror, she quickly looked away, but not before she caught the expression she'd seen earlier, when she'd been presented to him like a fully made-over doll.

That strange feeling stirred in her stomach again.

He doesn't want you.

And neither did she want him. She could never want someone so cruel.

When they reached the ground floor, he turned to her. 'Ready?'

'No.'

'Good.' Smiling broadly, he took her hand and led her out into the Manhattan night for the second time.

Her pulse kicked into life.

This was the first time he'd properly touched her skin other than that fleeting kiss earlier.

His hand was enormous, swallowing hers like a giant paw.

His driver was ready for them.

Thankful to be able to shake her hand out of Gabriele's so she could get into the open back door, she sat down and pressed her hands between her thighs, wiping away the moisture that had sprung on her palms.

They rode in silence, the darkened glass dividing them from his driver meaning they didn't have to fake conversation or adoration.

Traffic was lighter than the night before but it still took them twenty minutes to arrive at the restaurant Gabriele had chosen for them.

The second the driver opened her door, Elena knew her identity had been discovered.

Lights flashed in her face, blinding her with their brilliance.

Gabriele took charge, getting out first and marching through the waiting paparazzi, to take her hand. Placing a protective arm around her waist, he led her inside.

Totally unprepared for a siege, she shrank into him, horrified at such behaviour and the shouts being called out as the horde yelled questions about their relationship.

They were led straight to their table. When they were sitting down and facing each other, she was astonished to see a look of satisfaction on Gabriele's face.

'You *enjoyed* that?' she asked.

His eyes gleamed but there was a fury contained within them.

'I've dealt with much worse. And their presence here— they were waiting for us, in case you hadn't realised—guarantees that your father will have his morning coffee seeing pictures of you held in my arms.'

It was at that precise moment she understood Gabriele genuinely believed her father had set Alfredo up.

The hate he had for her family was built, at least in his own mind, on solid foundations.

He'd taken the rap to protect Alfredo but could not allow himself to believe in his father's guilt. He was in denial. Rather than accept the truth he'd pointed the finger at her father.

Which meant that Gabriele himself was innocent of the crimes he'd spent two years in prison for.

Was it possible he was right about Alfredo's innocence too...?

No, she couldn't believe that. Because that would mean he was right about her own father and she just could not believe her father would commit fraud and set his oldest friend up to take the fall.

She wasn't naïve enough to think her father had never cut corners in his life but what Gabriele was accusing him of?

No. It just couldn't be.

'Elena?'

His voice broke her out of her trance.

He leaned forward and murmured, 'Adoration, *tesoro*, adoration.'

Taking a deep breath to clear the unwarranted thoughts, she rested her chin on her hand and gazed at him.

And, as she stared into those soulful dark eyes, she couldn't help but think that should he be anyone other than he was—a vengeful blackmailer—looking at him with adoration would be no hardship at all.

Elena had been locked in the bathroom for so long Gabriele wondered if she'd drowned in the shower.

He had to give it to her; she'd performed admirably that night.

All evening she'd kept her eyes on his, fluttering her lashes, laughing and smiling. She'd even managed not to flinch too overtly whenever he'd taken her hand. No other diner in the restaurant would be in any doubt that they were a couple very much enjoying each other's company.

When Elena finally came out of the bathroom he wasn't surprised to find her wearing her oversized pyjamas rather than the sexy sleepwear Liana had selected for her and which she'd put away in her dressing room earlier with her other purchases.

'Do you have a preference to which side you like to sleep?' he asked from his vantage point in the middle of the bed.

She shook her head, shuffling with obvious trepidation to him.

'I'll take the right side, then.' He moved over.

Gingerly, she lifted the sheets and climbed in. As she did so he caught a whiff of minty toothpaste and a delicate floral scent.

There was an immediate thickening of his blood. And a thickening of another part of his anatomy.

She turned her back to him and burrowed under the sheets so only the top of her white-blonde hair showed.

Gabriele switched the bedside light off, plunging the room into darkness.

He gazed up at the ceiling, a hand resting above his head, and tried to empty his mind of clutter and not pay too much attention to the fact that Elena lay beside him.

Soon the stiffness in his loins would subside.

These were natural reactions for a man to have.

Sharing a bed with a pretty woman, even one clad in the most disgusting nightclothes he'd ever had the misfortune to see, would be enough to make any man hard, especially when that man had been celibate for the best part of four years.

After Sophia had ended their engagement, he'd smarted for a while but had been too caught up in the legal battle to allow himself to dwell on it for any length of time. Prison itself had been about getting through each day. Even with his work detail he'd had plenty of time to think and all that thinking had been spent on one thing—revenge. Sophia had hardly crossed his mind.

Since his release, the part of his brain not plotting his revenge had been spent rebuilding his and Mantegna Cars' reputation. This rebuilding would culminate in the car being launched to honour his father's memory. There simply hadn't been the space for a woman, not in any capacity.

So it was no wonder that lying in the dark next to Elena had made his libido jump-start itself.

They were on the front page of every major paper in the US and Europe.

The Burying of the Hatchet? screamed the most common variety of headline.

They were also the headliners of all the major news outlets on the Web and the top trending story on social media. The picture most commonly used in them had Gabriele's arm wrapped protectively around her and Elena's head resting against his chest.

While she'd been sleeping, her phone, put on silent for the night, had gone berserk. She awoke to eleven missed calls from her father and brothers. All their texts and emails were variants of 'call me now'.

There were also dozens of messages and missed calls from journalists and bloggers wanting comments on her relationship with Gabriele.

She couldn't bring herself to listen to the voicemails.

Turning her phone off, she climbed out of the empty bed

and headed to the bathroom, splashing some water on her face and brushing her teeth.

As with the day before, Gabriele was already showered and dressed. She found him in the dining room sipping a cup of coffee. He was casually dressed again, wearing black chinos and a grey T-shirt under an unbuttoned checked shirt with the sleeves rolled up.

An empty plate had been pushed to one side, half a dozen newspapers strewn before him.

'Good morning, *tesoro.*' He rose to his feet, a smile playing on his lips, one she was coming to recognise as the smile of satisfaction he gave when he was pleased with a plan coming to fruition.

To her shock, he stepped to her, pulled her into his arms and briefly covered her mouth with his own.

She reared her head back but couldn't break free from his hold. 'What are…?'

'We have company,' he interrupted in a low voice, dragging his lips across her cheek and dipping into her neck, his hand rubbing across her back.

'Come, have some breakfast,' he said in a normal tone, pulling the seat out from beside his own and virtually pressing her into it.

It was then that she saw the small man standing at the door separating the dining room from the kitchen.

'Michael, this is Elena,' Gabriele said by way of introduction, smiling affectionately at her as he took her stiff hand in his.

Michael bustled into the room, beaming widely. 'It's a pleasure to meet you, Miss Ricci.' He spoke with a strong New York drawl. 'What can I get you for breakfast?'

'Erm…'

'I can recommend his poached eggs.' Gabriele smoothed a strand of hair away from her cheek.

As soon as Michael had disappeared back into the kitchen, Elena snatched her hand from Gabriele's hold.

'There was no need for that,' she hissed.

'There was every need,' he answered, taking her hand back. 'You are like a cat on hot coals around me. We're going to the city clerk's office later to arrange our wedding licence. Tomorrow we marry. You need to be comfortable with me holding you and touching you.'

'I did all that last night,' she said indignantly, though making an effort to keep her voice down.

'No, you made a start last night,' he corrected. 'You were as stiff as a board under my touch but anyone would excuse that because of the paparazzi's presence. When we see the clerk, you have to keep in mind they deal with couples in love all the time. They will know a fake when they see it.'

'I am *trying*.'

'And I'm going to help you.'

'How?'

'By kissing you. Properly.'

Any objection she would have made was swept away when he placed his giant palms to her cheeks and brought his mouth to hers.

The couple of times he'd kissed her before had been the briefest of touches, a flash of warmth and then done, leaving nothing but the faintest impression on her lips and a trace of his masculine body heat.

This time...

His lips caressed hers, moving softly. His long fingers traced her cheeks then spread out to thread into her hair and massage into her scalp.

Gently but authoritatively his tongue slid out to probe and caress her lips, which were still clamped tightly together.

But she was fighting a losing battle.

As hard as she tried to keep a hold of herself, to stop this subtle erotic assault from seeping into her, all the tiny atoms inside her were awakening, sensation spreading through her.

What was happening to her?

And then her lips made the tiniest of partings that was enough for him to sweep his tongue into her mouth.

Deep, dark heat suffused her, his taste seeping into her. Coffee, the faint trace of mint and a taste she didn't recognise but she knew was his and his alone.

With shock, she suddenly realised her hand had moved of its own accord to rest on his shoulder, her fingers gripping it tightly.

And she was kissing him back. Her tongue had slipped into his mouth and was mimicking the explorations he was making in her own.

She flexed her fingers and let go, then reared her head back enough to break the kiss.

'That's enough,' she muttered in a voice that sounded distant. The only sound she could make out was the ringing in her ears.

Gabriele didn't say anything, his hold on her head still firm as he gazed intently into her eyes, the expression on his face making her stomach contract in on itself and her thundering heart crash painfully against her ribs.

Thank God Michael chose that moment to come back into the room with a pot of coffee, clearing his throat loudly to announce his presence.

Gabriele moved his hands from her hair and straightened.

'Your breakfast will be with you in five minutes,' Michael said, pouring her a cup and then leaving as quickly as he'd come.

Shaken, her body still singing, heat still swirling, she added a spoonful of sugar with a trembling hand.

Gabriele was her sworn enemy. She had no right to take such pleasure from his kiss.

She had no right to want more.

'That's much better,' he said with approval.

'Don't ever do that again.' She couldn't look at him.

'Don't pretend you didn't enjoy it.'

'Don't pretend that I did.' She hadn't *enjoyed* it. What she had felt—what she still felt—was something she hadn't known she *could* feel.

His voice dropped and he spoke into her ear, blowing more of that gorgeous heat over her sensitised skin. 'You taste like nectar. Soon, I will taste all of you.'

She wrapped her hands around her cup, breathing deeply, trying in vain to take control of herself.

His gaze stayed locked on her, penetrating her skin.

This man was her sworn enemy.

'What's the matter, *tesoro*? Does your desire for me scare you?'

'There is no desire. All I feel for you is loathing. All I want is for you to release me from this nightmare.'

Instead of being angry, he laughed. 'There is no shame in attraction. It is natural.'

Not for *her* it wasn't.

But she had no intention of sharing that with him. The contract she'd signed stipulated she gave him her body, not her thoughts. The only intimacies they would share would be in the bedroom and they would be as brief as humanly possible.

Gabriele got to his feet. 'I have some calls to make. Can you be ready to leave in an hour?'

Thrown at his abrupt change of conversation, she looked at him.

And immediately wished she hadn't.

Every time she looked at him her chest tightened some more.

Tomorrow she would marry this man.

She would belong to him.

And the only way to cut the bonds that would bind them was to give him the one thing she'd never given to anyone. Her body.

But the one thing she now knew above all else was that

she would never allow him to kiss her again. Not as he'd just done.

It made her feel too much.

Somehow Elena made it through their meeting with the official at the city clerk's office without incident. She'd held Gabriele's hand and smiled adoringly every time their eyes met. She'd even managed a simper.

The only time she'd come close to crumbling that day was when Gabriele had taken her to a boutique, leaving her with the instructions, 'You need to choose a dress to marry in. White. Nothing subversive.'

She'd thumbed through the many and varied beautiful dresses with a deep ache inside her.

She might never have expected to marry, but this…

This was an abomination. A mockery of everything marriage was supposed to stand for. She was marrying a man she despised and who loathed her with equal intensity.

You have to do it. If you don't, he'll destroy you all.

It was this thought that had sustained her through her chat with her father that evening, before she and Gabriele had sat down for a quiet meal prepared for them by the housekeepers.

Elena refused to give credence to Gabriele's belief that her father had framed Alfredo, yet it echoed in her head with every word exchanged between them. But she would not ask for her father's side. He had nothing to answer for.

It hurt so much to hear the strain in her father's voice, knowing his fears of his only daughter seeing a convicted criminal. He'd casually asked if she'd any plans to see 'Mantegna' again. She'd crossed her fingers and said in as cheerful a voice as she could muster, 'Oh, yes, Papà, he's such a lovely man.'

Now she lay beside that 'lovely man' feigning sleep.

This time tomorrow they would be married.

This time tomorrow she would no longer be a virgin.

Gabriele turned in his sleep. A warm leg brushed against her.

She stopped breathing.

Sensation spread throughout her, a low ache pulsing deep in her pelvis.

She gritted her teeth and exhaled through her mouth.

How could she be so aware of him? Why could her body not hate him with the same passion as her brain?

If she could only switch her body off she would be able to ignore the fact that sleeping beside her was the most physically attractive man she'd ever met.

She could pretend the heat suffusing her at his nearness meant nothing.

'Elena, are you ready?' Gabriele banged on the bedroom door, where she'd been holed up for the best part of an hour, telling him she wanted to be alone as she prepared.

The door swung open.

All she had on was a mauve robe. A towel was wrapped around her hair.

'I can't do it,' she said, panic in her voice.

'Do what?' He looked at his watch. His driver would be here any minute to take them to the Manhattan Marriage Bureau. Everything was set. All they had to do was turn up. If she was about to renege on their contract...

'My make-up,' she screeched. 'I can't remember what Adrian told me to do.'

Not only was there panic in her voice but in her eyes too.

She was so highly strung at that moment she could snap like a too taut piece of elastic.

'I'll be back in a minute,' he said.

'Where are you going?'

'One minute.' He went to his drinks cabinet and poured

two hefty measures of brandy, then carried the glasses back to the bedroom and pressed one in her hand.

'Drink it,' he commanded. 'It will calm your...'

She'd downed it before he could finish his sentence.

'Can I have another?'

'Sure.'

He went off and poured them both another. She drank it as quickly as the first and wiped her mouth with the back of her hand.

'Better?'

She nodded.

'Elena...' Her robe had opened a touch, enough for him to catch a glimpse of a small breast.

He blinked and refocused his attention on her face.

'Elena, we have plenty of time,' he lied. 'Just do your best. Everyone will be too busy looking at your dress to pay attention to your face.'

He'd waited in a nearby coffee shop while she'd bought it. He'd spent the time trying not to think of their breakfast kiss, the remnants of which had still lingered in his bloodstream. It *still* lingered.

Before his engagement to Sophia he'd had a steady stream of regular girlfriends. He would never have considered himself a playboy but he'd had a lot of fun. Then he'd turned thirty and decided it was time to settle down. It was what people did when they still had trust in human decency.

Now, there was no one alive he trusted and he never would again.

His father had trusted Ignazio. He'd never dreamed his oldest, closest friend would betray him in such a manner.

Gabriele had trusted Ignazio too. Why on earth would he not? But where had this trust got him? A prison sentence, a dead father and a severely incapacitated mother.

He'd trusted Sophia. She hadn't cared to believe in him, her only concern saving her reputation.

That was what trusting someone who wasn't your own blood got you. Pain.

When his time with Elena came to an end, he was sure he would date again—he wasn't *dead*—but sharing a life with anyone? Not a chance in hell.

At the time, Sophia had, on paper, seemed the perfect wifely candidate. They'd agreed on all the major things like religion and politics. It was the perfect meeting of minds. Plus she was from an old wealthy family so there was no question of her being a gold-digger. And she was beautiful. Properly beautiful. The kind of beauty that men and women alike would turn their heads to look at twice.

In the year he'd been with her, not one single kiss had elicited the reaction kissing Elena had evoked. He couldn't remember a single kiss that had ever provoked such a strong surge of heat not just through his loins but through his blood, his bones, his very flesh.

He'd sat in that coffee shop, talking quietly on the phone to the man who could clear his name, trying to think of the words to induce him into switching sides, but his concentration had hung by a thread. His blood had thrummed too deeply from his kiss with Elena to think clearly.

The desire it had provoked in him had been inexplicable. It still was. As he looked at her now, standing before him with nothing but a robe covering her, the urge to take her into his arms and carry her to the bed was strong.

But, as he told himself grimly, desire meant nothing. It didn't change anything.

But it would certainly make marriage to her more pleasurable.

She nodded, her lips pursed, determination etched on her face. 'I can do this.'

'Good. I'll leave you to get on.'

Closing the door behind him, he wondered what kind of woman made it to the age of twenty-five without knowing how to apply make-up. He'd always assumed it was something inbuilt in them, like their ability to multitask without breaking a sweat.

How sheltered *had* her life been?

He knew Ignazio had kept her in the home for much of her childhood. His own father had often commented on it, saying how sad it was that his friend was hiding his only daughter away while his sons roamed free. No wonder she had aspired to be as much like her brothers as she could.

She was a strong, confident woman now, he assured himself. Whatever kind of childhood she'd had, it didn't change who she had become.

Forty minutes later she finally appeared.

The dress she'd chosen to marry him in was white, as he'd stipulated, but that was the only truly traditional aspect. Sleeveless, it had a high lace neckline and fell like a fan above her knees. On her feet were simple white shoes with the tiniest of heels.

Her newly feathered fringe had been swept to one side, the rest of it gathered in her newly favoured knot at the back of her neck. She'd kept her make-up simple but effective.

'Well?' she demanded.

'It's perfect.' He nodded his approval. 'You've chosen well.'

'I couldn't bring myself to buy a floor-length traditional dress. It would have made this whole farce an even bigger mockery.'

'Quite,' he said sardonically, not liking the cramp of guilt that seized his gut.

Had Elena *wanted* a traditional marriage?

It wasn't something he'd cared to consider.

And now was not the moment to consider it. Whatever she'd hoped for was none of his concern.

Besides, if a large, cherub-filled church wedding rather than what was regarded as an *intimate elopement* was something she wanted, she could always do it with someone else once they were divorced.

Remembering the delivery that had come earlier, he strode to the table and removed the delicately tied white roses from the box.

'What are they for?' she asked with a puzzled frown, taking them from him and sniffing them.

'They're your bridal bouquet to hold as we exchange our vows.' As he spoke, he pinned a single white rose to the lapel of the blazer of his navy pinstriped suit. 'You didn't think your loving fiancé would forget such an important detail, did you?'

She smiled with poison-laced sweetness. 'As we're not bothering with an engagement ring, guests or a reception, I'm surprised you bothered.'

'But, my love, there will be photographers there to witness our joy when we leave the civic hall.'

'Let's hope they don't learn we spent the night before our wedding together, and that you saw me before we exchanged our vows. It would be dreadful if they were to say our wedding is doomed by bad luck before it's even started.'

'Then we must put on a worthy display of our love so those doubts never rear up. Don't you think?'

She tilted her head coquettishly and fluttered her eyelashes. 'But of course, my mouldy little acorn. Our love will shine through.'

'A mouldy little acorn?' God, she amused him. He had no idea why but she did.

And he had no idea why he experienced a pang to wonder what it would be like between them if they had met under entirely different circumstances...

CHAPTER SEVEN

THE THREE OTHER couples in the waiting room were bouncing with excitement.

Elena tried not to study them too overtly but their body language fascinated her. And saddened her.

These couples were happy. They were marrying with the best of intentions—for love. She was marrying to stop Gabriele from destroying her family.

She'd made her daily call to her father and had been utterly relieved when it had gone to voicemail. She'd left a message saying she would call tomorrow then switched her phone off.

It hurt to think how upset he would be to learn she'd married the man subtly poisoning minds against him.

Gabriele's enormous arm was around her, her head nestled carefully in its crook.

She could feel the thud of his heartbeat. She could smell that masculine fruity scent.

It felt far too good to allow herself—for the sake of their audience—to sink into his strength.

Michael and his wife, Lisa, were sitting beside them, the pair beaming, clearly delighted their boss was getting married.

Romantic was the word Lisa had used when they'd met them there.

An elopement to a register office was romantic?

Elena's parents had married in an old Tuscan church surrounded by hundreds of loved ones. The pictures in their official album had shown her father beaming with pride and her mother, dressed in a traditional floor-length white dress, glowing with happiness. Their love had shone through.

She had never expected to marry but in the back of her mind had always been the wistful imaginings of a big traditional wedding surrounded by people who loved her, and with happiness in her heart.

Not this. Nothing like this.

An official appeared, ready to lead the next couple to the room in which they would legitimise their relationship.

It was *their* turn.

Ice filtered through her veins, freezing her bottom to her seat.

Gabriele helped her to her feet and pulled her to him.

'Ready to become Mrs Mantegna?' he murmured, rubbing his nose against hers, a warning in his eyes.

Aware of happy gazes upon them drinking in their devotion, she pressed her lips lightly to his.

'I hate you so much,' she breathed.

She could only assume it was a form of punishment that made him dart his tongue into her mouth and kiss her with such possessiveness that she had to cling to him to keep herself upright.

Her legs turned to jelly, her stomach to goo and she had to fight with everything she had not to take pleasure from it… Except she did. Every part of her body took pleasure from it.

Done; his eyes gleamed before he turned to the official and said, 'Lead the way.'

Five minutes later they were husband and wife.

They left the building into a blaze of afternoon sunlight, the rays bouncing off the elegant gold band now firmly placed on Elena's wedding finger. It had surprised her that Gabriele had chosen to wear one too.

The handful of photographers who pitched themselves outside the building in the hope of business from those marrying on the spur of the moment had tripled in numbers.

The paparazzi had arrived.

No guessing who had tipped them off.

Hands clasped, they posed but refused to make any comment.

A crowd of curious well-wishers began to surround them, snaps from phones being taken at all angles and directions.

Michael and Lisa, trailing behind, spoke only to say of their happiness for them, then left in a cab, en route to the airport, where they would be taking a two-week holiday courtesy of Gabriele.

When enough pictures had been taken, they fought their way through the crowd that had grown to epic proportions and got into the back of Gabriele's waiting car.

Elena would bet anything the snaps of them had been beamed around the world before they'd turned the corner of the block.

'Don't you want to go out and celebrate?' she asked with only a small amount of sarcasm. 'I've never known of a marriage without a big feast and party afterwards.'

'This is New York. Marriages here come in many different flavours.' He grinned, his eyes glittering. 'We will return to my apartment and celebrate privately.'

She didn't answer. She couldn't.

What was the point in arguing? It would only delay the inevitable.

There was no backing out. That avenue was closed. She'd married Gabriele knowing full well that when she signed the marriage licence it cemented her commitment to sleep with him.

The worst of it all was knowing that she *wanted* it to happen.

Her fear was enormous but the thrill of anticipation equalled it.

There had been a moment in the night when she'd awoken from one of her intermittent dozes to find her face close enough to feel his breath on her skin. The *longing* she had experienced in those few semi-conscious moments...

She'd wanted to kiss him.

It had shocked her. It still did.

She cleared her throat before speaking. 'I assumed you would want to throw a big party to show the world you own me now.'

'I thought you said I would never own you?' he said, his tone lightly mocking. 'But yes, I am ahead of you on that—Anna Maria is organising a party in Florence for all our family and friends to attend two weeks on Saturday. The invites will be sent tomorrow.'

'Will my family be invited?'

'*Our* family,' he corrected. 'We're married now so your family is mine and mine is yours and they will all be invited.' His grin remained fixed but his eyes were hard. 'I'm very much looking forward to seeing them again.'

'I'll bet you are.'

He leaned closer to her and took her hand, bringing it to his lips. 'It will be an evening of celebration but that is for another day. Right now my attention is on an altogether more pleasurable occurrence.'

Elena had stopped breathing, her fingers tingling with sensation where his breath whispered against it.

How could she respond so physically to him? By any law of logic and decency, it shouldn't be possible.

And how could her body buzz with the thought of what the night would bring?

They'd arrived back at his apartment.

Gabriele let go of her hand but instead of getting out, he brushed his lips against hers, catching her unawares, not giving her time to turn her face away. 'Come, Mrs Mantegna, let us celebrate our new union.'

The atmosphere in the elevator to Gabriele's apartment was as charged as he'd ever known it, as if an electrical current had been looped around them, pulling them ever closer together.

'Let's get a drink,' he said, leading her into the dining room.

She stepped through the door and came to an abrupt halt.

'Did you do this?' she asked.

On the table were two bottles of pink champagne in a bucket and two flutes. Next to them were silver trays of Italian and American canapés and sweet treats, from asparagus wrapped in Parma ham, to delicate pastry bites to heart-shaped chocolate truffles. Somewhere in those delicious-looking trays of food lurked a bite or two laced with real truffles—he could smell the distinct musky, nutty scent, an aroma that brought to mind memories of his childhood before they'd emigrated, when he and his father had spent a day truffle detecting.

He had so many happy memories of his father. A childhood filled with happiness. But that was all he had left. Memories.

'A private feast for two,' he murmured, slipping an arm around her waist and pressing into her back.

There was the lightest of pressure returned to him before she jolted forward to the table. 'Well, thank you for this because I am starving.'

'That'll teach you to skip breakfast.'

She met his eyes. Her cheeks coloured and she looked away.

Gabriele hid a smile.

The anticipation of the consummation of their vows had given an added piquancy to their mutual loathing. He could almost taste it.

There wasn't the slightest doubt in his mind that the attraction was reciprocated. None at all. He could see it in her colouring, hear it in the deepening of her breaths. And, most of all, he could still feel the kisses they'd shared. And they *had* shared them. She'd kissed him right back.

'Take a seat,' he said, pulling a chair out for her. While she sat and began unwrapping the trays of food, he took a bottle of the champagne, aimed it at the wall, and uncorked it.

He poured them both a glass and passed one to her.

Raising his glass in the air, he said, 'To us.'

She chinked her glass to his.

'To us,' she echoed, before adding, 'And here's to as short a marriage as it's possible to have.'

'And may all those short days be as pleasurable as they can be,' he retorted, enjoying watching the colour rise back up her cheeks again.

For all her words of being starving, Elena only nibbled at the spread before her.

Gabriele, never one to turn down food, found his own appetite strangely diminished too.

It had been a long time since he'd been with a woman, he reasoned. The expectation must be affecting him more than he'd expected. All the same, he ate over half the available food and a handful of the truffles.

He was content to let the meal drag out and make idle chit-chat. There was no rush. They had all night.

He almost laughed. A piece of paper they'd both signed that day said they had the rest of their lives.

When the first bottle of champagne was empty, he reached for the one sitting in the ice bucket.

'I don't want another drink,' Elena said suddenly, her eyes on him. 'I'm ready to go to bed.'

He raised a brow, a thrill racing through him at her admission.

Colour crept over her cheeks but she held his gaze, searching his eyes as intently as he searched hers. He brushed his thumb down the length of her cheekbone, marvelling at the softness of her skin. Her eyes closed and when she opened them the green darkened and a spark flashed from them.

'I'm ready for bed,' she repeated in a whisper.

* * *

Elena felt so tightly wound that she fleetingly wondered if she would be sick.

She'd hardly eaten a thing, the butterflies in her stomach fluttering too madly to let anything else in. With every passing minute of their shared meal she'd expected Gabriele to take charge, declare their meal over, and lead her into the bedroom. That he had been happy to linger had only added to the fear and anticipation rioting together in her. It had been like a ticking clock, the pendulum swinging louder and louder with every beat until it had become too much to bear.

She hadn't been able to take the suspense a moment longer.

Being the one to vocalise it had felt, strangely, empowering. She had made the first move. She'd taken the power out of his hands and claimed it for herself.

And now the butterflies had gone berserk, the fear being crowded out.

God forgive her, she *wanted* him. She wanted this to happen.

But she would only give him her body. Her head and emotions belonged only to her and she would keep them firmly detached. Men did it all the time so why should she be any different?

All the same, it took a few moments to get her feet moving out of the bathroom.

Gabriele was already propped up in bed, waiting for her, his broad chest bare.

His eyes shimmered to see her. He turned the sheets over beside him.

Under those same sheets she knew the rest of him was naked too. Just as she was naked beneath her silk robe.

The summer sun was still making its late descent, casting the room with a dusky hue. She wished it were fully dark; was certain it would make her feel a little less vulnerable.

She got under the sheets and lay on her back, pulling the sheets up to her shoulders.

Gabriele propped himself on an elbow and stared down at her. Unable to help herself, she gazed back.

Those soulful dark eyes swirled as if magma had been poured into them, an intensity there that made her heart skip and her nerves tauten painfully. Excitement and fear collided but she couldn't look away.

A large, warm hand rested on her collarbone, fingers tracing across to dip under her robe and begin the trail down to her belly, peeling the fabric back until he reached the knotted sash.

His eyes holding hers, still propped up on his elbow, he untied it.

Elena's heart hammered so hard its beats echoed in her ears. Breathing had become difficult, the air sticking in her throat. The line on her skin where his fingers had traced had been marked by his touch, the tingles spreading out through her flesh.

When Gabriele dipped his head and moved his mouth to hers, she only just turned her head away in time.

He stilled and gazed at her with questioning eyes before a half smile formed on his face.

'Ah,' he murmured softly, kissing her neck. 'This is where you make a show of doing your duty and nothing more.' He caught her earlobe in his teeth while he pulled her robe apart, exposing her breasts to him.

He gazed at them then looked back in her eyes, the magma in his pulsing. Gently he cupped her breast and stroked the puckered nipple with his thumb.

She closed her eyes as sensation rippled through her.

'We both know your desire for me is as strong as my desire for you,' he whispered, his mouth back at her ear, more sweet, sweet sensation skittering on her skin, under her skin, everywhere...

Gabriele shifted off his elbow and raised himself to kneel over her thigh. The movement shrugged the sheets off him, exposing more of the dark hair that covered his chest, down to his abdomen, thickening at his groin, where...

She blinked in shock.

She might have zero experience in this but even she could tell he was fully erect and hugely so.

A dull throb set off low within her, becoming altogether heavier and more heated when he pressed another kiss into her neck. And another. And another, drifting lower, down the valley of her breasts and over to capture a nipple in his mouth.

She couldn't contain the gasp that flew from her mouth.

The urge to touch him back grew from nowhere, and she grabbed at the ends of her pillow, clumping them in her fists.

This was too much. And yet, not enough.

Lightly, he traced his fingers over her skin, making swirls over her belly, his movement unhurried; lazy. Sensation was everywhere.

When he trailed a hand down her body and dipped a finger into her most intimate area, she clenched her teeth, still determined not to react. But *this*...in a place she'd never even touched herself...

Now he was the one to groan, a deep sound that came from the base of his throat, more like a growl from a wild animal than anything human.

'You really are exquisite.' He rested the palm of his hand so it covered the heart of her pleasure and slid another finger inside her.

Her breaths shortened.

The friction of his palm on her and the wholly unknown sensations being set off by the magic of his fingers...the battle to keep her head was being lost and she held the pillow even more tightly lest she give in and flatten her hands onto his back and feel the skin for herself and see if it felt as smooth beneath her fingertips as it seemed to her eye.

She would not give in. No matter how desperate a fight it would be.

But she was helpless to prevent the moan that left her mouth like a whimper.

'Admit that you want me,' Gabriele said hoarsely into her throat, his breath sending more sensation over her skin. 'I need to hear it.'

How could she deny it? Her body betrayed how much she desired him, reacting to his touch as if it were heaven-sent.

'Yes, I want you,' she whispered fiercely.

He groaned at her whispered admittance and moved fully between her thighs and took hold of himself, guiding himself to the place he'd just been touching her.

His erection pressed into her opening and then there was a sharp lance of pain as he drove inside her with one long, determined thrust.

Elena sucked in air and froze, so stunned at the sudden feel of him inside—fully, massively inside her—that she couldn't move.

Gabriele stopped moving too.

'Elena?'

His eyes, which hadn't left her face, now reflected stark shock.

After long moments passed in which nothing more was said but understanding flowed, he lowered himself to rest his weight on her, not enough to crush but enough that his entire upper body rested upon her, the darks hairs on his chest bristling against her breasts, his groin now resting against hers.

And, God, he was still inside her.

He was a part of her.

'Put your arms around me,' he said quietly.

The shock had gone from his eyes. Now there was something else there, a tenderness that made her lungs close even tighter.

Her fingers uncurled from the pillow of their own accord. At that moment Elena wasn't capable of rational thought. She wrapped her arms lightly around his back.

His skin felt so *smooth*.

'Breathe,' he whispered. He placed his forearms either side of her head and captured locks of her hair in his fingers. 'Breathe.'

She tried, drawing in choked air.

'Breathe.'

He moved inside her gently, his eyes holding hers, his hands stroking her hair.

'Move with me,' he said in that same low tone.

'I…' She didn't know how.

He must have understood.

A thumb brushed along her cheekbone. 'Do whatever feels good for you.'

He moved again, pulling out a little then pushing slowly back. 'Move with me,' he urged.

She raised her thighs a little and immediately the friction deepened.

His jaw clenched but his eyes were open, feeding her messages that there was nothing to be afraid of. Slowly, very slowly, he increased the movements.

From all Elena knew of sex, it was something to be hurried, a carnal event for the man to take his pleasure and for the woman to endure.

She had never known it could be tender.

She had never imagined *Gabriele* could be tender. But he was. His only concern was her pleasure and making this as good for her as it could be.

A swell of something she couldn't discern grew inside her chest and her fingers dug into the planes on his back, feeling the muscles beneath the smoothness.

Instinct took over and she found herself moving with him, hesitantly at first but with slow-increasing confidence, meeting his still-restrained thrusts as her body adjusted to these wonderful sensations spreading through her.

And they were wonderful. Like nothing she could ever have imagined.

The pulsations that had been building in her core grew stronger. Gabriele rocked gently in her, letting her have control of the tempo and strength. She raised her thighs a touch more, deepening the effect, and pressed herself tightly against him, locking her cheek next to his, feeling his hot breath on her skin.

And then she was crying out as the swelling exploded within her, rippling through every part of her with a strength that made her cling even tighter to him for support.

Through the heavenly yet shocking delight of what she was experiencing, Elena heard Gabriele's breathing deepen.

He whispered endearments, coaxing her to ride the waves until he let out a ragged groan and gave one last, lengthy thrust.

And then he collapsed on her.

With his face in her neck, his hands still running through her hair and the thunder of his heart echoing through her skin, Elena gazed at the ceiling, too shocked at what she had just experienced to think coherently or attempt to wriggle out from beneath him. The weight of his body on her and the heat of his breath in her neck…

Had that really just happened?

A strange lethargy crept through her sensitised body and a lump formed in her throat.

A lifetime of listening to her brothers and their friends discuss women with what amounted to contempt, and witnessing them treat the women in their lives as mere possessions, had convinced her that sex was a tool for men to assert their dominance. She'd assumed the phrase *making love* was from the realm of movies.

She hadn't been prepared for Gabriele to be so tender and gentle with her.

Even now that it was over, she would have assumed he would roll off her, let out a snore and, job done, go to sleep. She hadn't thought he would continue to caress her as if she mattered in any way; and this man was her enemy.

She hadn't expected to feel so *close* to him.

She could only imagine how he would make love if he was actually in love with the woman in his bed.

With that bitter thought, she finally psyched herself to move out from beneath him. He obliged, shifting his weight off her so she could roll onto her side and turn her back to him.

She could feel his eyes upon her, and waited for the dissection of what had just occurred to begin.

Instead, he hooked an arm around her waist and pulled her back so she was spooned against him.

Inexplicably, her eyes filled with tears. She blinked them away.

This was what she'd signed up for, she reminded herself for the umpteenth time.

Just because having sex with Gabriele had been the most incredible, fulfilling experience of her life didn't change any of the facts about him or them.

Yet, with his warmth permeating through her and his strength cocooning her, she drifted into sleep with a contentment in her limbs she had never known she could have.

CHAPTER EIGHT

GABRIELE PAUSED IN the doorway of the bedroom and peered at Elena's sleeping form.

The sheets looked as if she'd been wrestling them, a leg hooked around them, her arms thrown outwards.

He'd slept fitfully, waking half a dozen times, not touching her, just gazing at her with a chest so tight breathing was painful.

Staring at her now, he still couldn't comprehend that she'd been a virgin.

A virgin.

She shuffled and then raised her head. Opening a bleary eye, she stared at him for a moment before saying, 'What time is it?'

He looked at his watch. 'Six o'clock.'

Sitting up, she brushed her hair away from her face and hugged the sheets to her. 'Have you been working out?'

He looked down at his shorts and T-shirt and the training shoes still on his feet. 'What gave it away?'

The glimmer of a smile played on her lips.

'I went for a jog around Central Park.' Always up before the birds, that morning he'd risen even earlier, which was hardly surprising as they'd both fallen asleep in the early evening. 'Are you hungry?'

She rested her chin on her knees and nodded, almost shyly.

'I'm going to take a quick shower then I'll get some breakfast for us. Any requests?'

She shook her head.

She was so clearly ill at ease that for a moment his chest

constricted. He took a deep breath. 'Go back to sleep. I'll wake you when breakfast's ready.'

Not answering, she lay back down and curled the sheets around her.

Gabriele showered and dressed quickly, then went back out into the early Manhattan sun.

This was his favourite time of the day. In prison, early mornings had been filled with noise and activity. Here, in the open city streets, he could be on a different planet. There were people around—of course there were, this city never slept—but there was a stillness about them, as if they were robots charging themselves to alertness.

The welcoming scent of fresh donuts greeted him in his favourite deli one block from his apartment.

While he waited for his order to be done, he found his mind replaying everything from last night with Elena, just as it had while he'd jogged. Normally jogging cleared his mind of everything, allowing him to start the day afresh. Today...

One thing he had determined during his run was that he couldn't allow Elena's virginity to cloud his opinions or the route they were taking. She was still Ignazio's daughter. She was still up to her neck in his criminal doings and had played a hand in setting his father up. It was inconceivable that she wasn't involved.

Just because she'd been an innocent in one respect did not mean she was innocent in any other.

He would not allow himself to be derailed from his ultimate mission: the exoneration of his and his father's good names.

With that thought fortifying him, Gabriele took their breakfast and strolled back to the apartment block. While he waitedfor the elevator, his phone buzzed. It was a number he didn't recognise.

Putting the bag of food and coffee on a marble table in

the foyer, he hit the reply button and pressed the phone to his ear. *'Ciao?'*

'Mantegna?'

The voice on the other end was music to his ears. It was the voice he'd been waiting for.

'Ricci?'

'Is it true? Have you married my daughter?'

'Elena and I married yesterday afternoon—'

'You son-of-a—'

'It was a spur-of-the-moment thing,' Gabriele continued cordially as if Ignazio hadn't interrupted him, raising his hand to wave at the familiar face of a neighbour. 'We'll be having a party in a couple of weeks to celebrate. Your invitation will be posted today.'

The invitations would have the words 'Mr and Mrs Mantegna' emblazoned in large italics on them.

'What the hell are you playing at messing around with her?' Ignazio demanded, his tone full of menace.

Good. This was the reaction he wanted. Ignazio was wounded. He was also under threat. People under threat were more likely to make mistakes.

If Ignazio had any idea Gabriele was attempting to lure one of his most trusted aides away too…

'Elena and I are not playing at anything.' He didn't care if Ignazio believed in his love. All Gabriele cared was that Ignazio believed Elena had fallen in love with him. 'Elena loves me.'

He could hear heavy breathing down the phone, the sound of a man who'd smoked far too many cigarettes in his life fighting to control his temper.

'If you hurt her, I'll kill you.'

'Why would I hurt her?' He thought back to the shyness in her eyes when she'd awoken a short while ago. He remembered the breathlessness of her cries as she'd come in his arms.

'I mean it.' The voice was threatening but Gabriele detected an underlying tinge of panic.

Oh, this was *very* good.

Was this concern for his daughter or concern that Gabriele's access in the family had made Ignazio vulnerable?

He put him on the spot. 'Why do you think I would hurt your daughter?'

Ignazio didn't answer for the longest time. Gabriele could almost hear his brain ticking as he thought up an answer that wouldn't incriminate him.

When he finally answered, all he said was, 'Elena is nothing to do with anything.'

'Elena is my wife. She belongs to me now and I don't hurt what's mine.'

Terminating the call, he switched the phone to silent and stuck it in his back pocket.

Grabbing their breakfast, he got into the elevator and pressed the button for his floor, waiting for some form of euphoria to strike.

Ignazio was wounded. In the grand scheme of things it was a minor victory but one he had fully expected to relish.

Instead, he felt flat.

Back in the apartment he found Elena in the kitchen emptying the trays of food from the day before into a bin. As she leaned forward, her pert bottom, clad in black cropped trousers, curved for his eyes to appreciate.

After four years of celibacy he wasn't surprised to find that one bout of lovemaking had reignited his libido. What he hadn't expected was the strength.

She cast him a quick glance before tipping the remnants of the last tray in the bin. With a round-necked black and white striped fitted T-shirt, her damp hair loose around her shoulders and her face free from make-up, she looked as innocent as he knew she'd physically been only the day before.

'I've brought bagels and coffee.' He placed his wares on the kitchen table.

'Go ahead. I'll just be a minute.' She didn't look at him, intent on her clean-up mission. She moved to the sink, which she'd filled with soapy water, and dunked their champagne flutes into it.

'There's no need to do that. There's a cleaner coming in later.'

'It's therapeutic.'

'Elena, sit down and eat.'

She stood rigid at the sink then turned to join him, taking a seat at the far end of the table from him.

He watched as she ate, chewing slowly with each mouthful as if it were a chore that needed to be fulfilled.

'Did it not cross your mind to tell me you were a virgin?' he asked casually.

Her hand hovered in mid-air before she put her half-eaten bagel down. 'No.'

'You didn't think I had a right to know?'

'No.'

'Why not?'

She fixed cold eyes on him, so different from the shock that had reflected from them when he'd thrust into her that first time and so different from the wonder that had resonated when she'd come in his arms.

To discover the woman in his arms had been a virgin, that it was her first time...

The desire that had brimmed inside him, on the brink of boiling point as he'd plunged inside her, had notched down to an immediate simmer. The significance of what he had just done had hit him with full force.

From feeling as if he would explode, his only concern had been that she was okay, to soothe her, to wipe away the discomfort he knew that first thrust had given her.

Her response had been mind-blowing. Slowly, shyly, she had come alive in his arms.

'Did I hurt you?'

She shrugged. 'A little.'

'I'm sorry.' Sorrier than he could ever express.

Another shrug.

'If you'd told me, I would have been gentle.'

Something softened in her gaze before she looked away and said quietly, 'You *were* gentle.'

'I would have been gentle from the outset.' He took a drink from his coffee. 'I'm not going to lie to you, you are a very sexy woman. I haven't been with anyone in four years…'

Her eyes snapped back to him.

'…and I was like an over-eager panther. You should have told me.' He shook his head, still incredulous. 'Why?'

The softening of her features hardened again. 'Why was I a virgin?'

'Yes.'

'Honestly? If I'd had my way I would have remained a virgin until I died. Men are pigs and I knew I would never meet one who didn't conform to that opinion.'

He winced, wishing he could stick up for his gender but knowing he was in no position to offer a defence, not after he'd effectively blackmailed her into giving her virginity to him.

She drained her coffee and pushed her plate to one side. 'For all that, I do need to thank you.'

'For what?'

'For showing me that just because a man is a pig out of the bedroom doesn't mean he isn't capable of tenderness in it. I *should* have told you but I didn't think it would make any difference to how you treated me. I can see now that I was wrong.' The faintest trace of colour covered her cheeks but she carried on. 'It wasn't as bad as I thought it would be.'

Something swelled inside him that, for once, wasn't in his groin. 'Are you paying me a compliment?'

A smile ghosted her lips. 'Let's not get carried away. You can call it faint praise.'

'Then this afternoon it will be my mission to move on from faint praise to full-blown applause.' He didn't add that right at that moment he would happily pull her onto his lap and take her again.

Elena being a virgin put a whole new level of complexity on their physical relationship and he had to respect that sex and everything that went with it was new for her.

A thrill raced through him to think that *he* would be the one to teach her the art of pleasure.

'This afternoon?' Her eyes flashed. 'Won't we be travelling?'

'Our flight is scheduled for two p.m. We'll have ten whole hours to keep ourselves amused before we land in Florence.'

'I'll be sure to bring a good book with me, then,' she said with a husky catch in her voice.

The temptation to just pull her into his arms and take her grew stronger but he tempered it.

'We'll be leaving in an hour,' he said. 'Will you be ready?'

She nodded.

'Good. We're making a detour on the way to the airport.'

'Oh?'

'We're going to visit my mother. It's time for her to meet her new daughter-in-law.'

Elena gazed at the sprawling white ranch-type house on the fringe of New Jersey's Somerset County.

'What a pretty house,' she said, stepping out of the car and shielding her eyes from the brilliance of the sun. After the bustle of Manhattan the silence was stark. 'Did you live here?'

He nodded. 'My parents bought it when we first emigrated.'

'How old were you?'

'Ten.'

'What was that like for you? Was it hard moving to a new country?' The gravelled pathway crunched beneath her leather Roman-style sandals.

'It was fun.' He grinned but the apprehension that had lined his face on the long car journey was still there. 'My parents made it into a big adventure for me.'

They'd reached the steps to the front porch. Gabriele paused before climbing them. 'You remember I told you my mother has dementia?'

She nodded warily. She hadn't broached the subject on the drive over because she still smarted that he held her partly responsible for his mother's condition.

There was no way to prove a negative and, with his opinion of her so deeply entrenched, she knew that mere words would never convince him of her innocence.

In Gabriele's eyes, his father was Snow White to her father's Evil Queen.

'Just…' He sighed, shook his head and opened the door. 'Hello?' he called out, walking through a large reception room.

A large woman wearing jeans and a plain white top came out of a door. She beamed to see him.

'Gabriele, how lovely to see you,' she said in Italian. She looked at Elena, who was trying to hide behind him. 'And this must be your wife.'

There was a quizzical expression on her face that told Elena this woman knew exactly who she was.

'She is,' he said, stepping aside and taking Elena's hand. 'This is Elena. Elena, this is Loretta, my mother's nurse. How is she today?'

'Not too bad. I'd say this is a medium day.' Loretta opened a door for them and walked up a wide corridor with stained-wood flooring.

They were taken into a spacious and airy living room.

Sitting in a reclining chair by the window watching television sat a frail-looking woman with white hair.

Loretta went to her and crouched down. 'Silvia, look, you have guests.'

The white hair turned slowly and a pale wrinkled face stared at them blankly.

Elena swallowed back her shock. She knew Gabriele's mother could be no older than mid-sixties but she looked decades older.

Then a spark of recognition flashed on the too-old face and Silvia got to her feet.

Loretta was there to take her arm and assist as she shuffled over to them.

To Elena's alarm, the recognition on Silvia's face wasn't directed at Gabriele but at herself.

'Hilde,' she cried. 'I knew you would come.'

Hilde?

Elena's blood stopped flowing.

Dimly she was aware of Gabriele and Loretta exchanging glances.

'I've made a room up for you,' Silvia continued. 'And Ginny... Jenny... Oh, what's her name? She has made us meatballs. Italian, not Swedish,' she added with a cackle.

With a start Elena understood.

Hadn't Gabriele said their mothers had been good friends?

Silvia thought she was her mother.

Having only photographs to go on, Elena knew she had a strong resemblance to her mother. She hadn't realised how stark the resemblance actually was.

Silvia now seemed to notice Gabriele. 'Hilde, you've brought a friend.'

What did she do? Did she tell this elderly woman who thought she was living in a time over two decades before that she was wrong?

But looking in those large brown eyes, so like her son's,

and the happiness emanating from them, she knew to tell the truth would be a cruelty she couldn't inflict.

Elena swallowed before reaching out to take Silvia's hand.

'This is Gabriele,' she said quietly. 'Do you remember him?'

Silvia scrunched her eyes to peer closely at him. 'No.' Something clouded in her eyes and she dropped her voice to a whisper. 'Does Ignazio know you've brought a man here?'

Something in her tone set Elena's heart thumping. 'He knows.'

'Good.' Silvia's fingers closed around her hand. She could feel the tremors in them.

'Shall we sit down?' Elena suggested. 'I'm very tired from the drive here.'

'I'll get us refreshments. Wine? I've got a bottle of that... oh, what's it called?...that red wine you like?'

'Coffee will be fine.'

'I'll sort refreshments out,' Loretta cut in with a smile.

Silvia peered at the nurse. 'Do I know you?'

Between them, they got Silvia back in her seat and pulled an armchair close to her for Elena to sit on.

Gabriele sat on the sofa, elbows on his knees, watching them.

'Alfredo never said you were coming,' Silvia now said, leaning towards Elena.

'It must have slipped his mind.'

Somehow they managed to talk, not an easy task what with Elena pretending to be her long-dead mother and Silvia forgetting words and losing threads of the conversation.

Loretta had brought coffee and biscuits in to them and then disappeared.

Gabriele made no attempt to join in their muddled talk but she could feel him sitting there, observing them.

She could only imagine how he must feel, his mother

talking animatedly to a complete stranger while failing to recognise her own son.

The only moment when Elena thought she might crack was when Silvia suddenly said, 'They told me you were dead.'

She swallowed back the shock and answered weakly, 'I was ill.'

'What was it again? Not the breast thing?'

'No. Not cancer. Septicaemia.' Her mother had cut her finger while gardening. The wound had become infected. After five days in hospital being pumped with every antibiotic known to man, her organs had failed and she'd died.

'I told Alfredo; Hilde would never be dead. She wouldn't leave her boys and that little girl. What's her name again?'

'Elena.'

'That's it. Elena. Such a pretty name. Did you get the dress we sent to her?'

'It's beautiful,' she said by way of an answer.

'Oh, yes. You sent a picture.' She craned her neck around the room before fixing on Gabriele. 'Alfredo, can you get the book for me? Hilde wants to see the pictures.'

Not by a word or expression did he react to being addressed by his dead father's name, quietly leaving the room as she'd asked.

When he returned it was with a thick, old-fashioned leather-bound photo album.

'Here's the book you wanted,' he said gently, placing it on the small table beside her.

'Did I? We wanted wine, didn't we, Hilde? That nice red wine you like.'

'I'll see if I can find a bottle.' He threw a quick wink at Elena that was tinged with sadness.

Elena gave him a sympathetic smile, then looked at the album. Her heart thumped. 'May I?'

He nodded.

With Silvia now off on a tangent discussing swimming pools, Elena opened the album.

It looked as if the photos had been taken shortly after the Mantegnas emigrated. Gabriele couldn't have been much older than ten in them. There he was, sitting on an old sofa with his father in this very room. Identical grins beamed for the camera.

She went through it all discreetly, still keeping up the conversation with Silvia, who had now moved on to talking about a programme Elena had never heard of but which she tried her hardest to pretend was a favourite.

More pictures. A summer barbecue. Gabriele's eleventh birthday.

And then she turned the page and her heart stopped.

That was her father, sitting next to Alfredo, arms around each other, at a large dining table strewn with empty wine bottles.

There were her three older brothers, all sitting under a Christmas tree opening presents. Gabriele was sitting with them. All four were wearing oversized Santa hats.

And there was her mother, laughing. A white-blonde toddler sat upon her lap with her own oversized Santa hat covering half her face.

Another of her mother, this time with a woman who had to be Silvia. They were in the kitchen, glasses of wine in hand.

A group picture of the five Mantegna and Ricci children huddled together on the sofa. She peered even harder. That was Gabriele whose lap she had been sat upon…

Elena thought she might faint.

She had been in this house before. She had eaten and slept under this roof.

When she could finally tear her eyes away from the pictures, Gabriele was watching her, his brow knotted in a question.

All she could do was shake her head.

Gabriele took control and got to his knees before his mother. He took her hands in his. 'Hilde and I need to leave now.'

'Are you taking her home?'

'Yes. I will bring her back soon.'

'Does Ignazio know?' This time, as Silvia said the name, something clouded on her face. Her voice was confused as she asked, 'Is he in prison?'

'No.'

'But soon,' she said decisively. She placed a shaking hand to her son's cheek. 'He will go there soon, Gabriele. You promised me.'

He kissed the hand then kissed her on both cheeks and her forehead. 'I promise you, Ignazio Ricci is paying for his sins.'

Silvia insisted on seeing them out. Leaning heavily on her nurse's arm, she waved and said, 'Goodbye, Veronica.'

She didn't say goodbye to Gabriele.

Shaken to her core and feeling as if she'd just spent two hours on an emotional roller coaster with no brakes, Elena walked like a zombie with Gabriele back to his car, where his driver was waiting for them, leaning against the car smoking a cigarette.

Nothing was said until they crossed the county line and she quietly asked, 'Who's Veronica?'

'My mother's sister. She died ten years ago.'

'Is she always like this?'

'Yes. Some days are better than others but she rarely knows who I am any more.' He gave a deep sigh. 'She's lost to me now. Sometimes I struggle to remember how she was before.'

Impulse made her take his hand and squeeze it. However difficult she'd found it, she could only imagine how hard it had been for him. This was his mother regarding the man she'd given birth to as a stranger. It had only been at the end of their visit that she'd been able to grasp who he was for a few fleeting moments. And their talk of prison...that had been about her father. Silvia, in her one lucid moment, had asked if Ignazio was in prison.

Gabriele's eyes were dull but his lips curved a little as he said a quiet, 'Thank you for being so kind to her.'

A lump formed in her throat. 'I'm just so sorry that she is the way she is.'

His smile was rueful. 'Until the dementia set in she was the liveliest woman you could meet. She had an opinion about everything.'

'Do you see her much?'

'As much as I can. When I was released from prison I wanted to bring her back to Italy to live with me there but the doctors said it would be too distressing for her.' He shrugged a massive shoulder. 'I visit every couple of weeks and make sure to stay a weekend every month.'

'Don't feel guilty,' she said, picking up on his tone. 'You've got a global business to run. It can't be easy juggling it all.'

'It would be easier if I had siblings—there would be more of us to pitch in and spend time with her. But she has Loretta who lives in during the week and a weekend nurse. And she has many friends who take it in turns to visit and keep her company. I'm lucky that I can afford to bring the help to her rather than put her in a home.'

'And she's very lucky to have you.'

Feeling a growing tightness in her chest, she carefully moved her hand away and placed it on her lap.

She didn't want to feel empathy for him but how could she not? When all was said and done, Gabriele was human and this was his mother trapped in a past that had long gone.

But she shouldn't feel that she wanted to wrap him in her arms and hold him close, to smooth his hair and stroke his skin.

'It was good of you to pretend to be your mother. That couldn't have been easy.'

She gave a jerk of her head. 'When you said they'd been close friends... I hadn't realised how close they were. And I had no idea I'd been to your family home—I didn't know I'd even been to America. I thought the first time I came here was a few years ago.'

'Before we moved to America our mothers were insep-arable. Our two families were incredibly close.' A smile tugged at his lips. 'I remember your christening.'

'You were *there*?'

'I think I was nine or ten. It was shortly before we emi-grated, which is probably why I remember it. Did you know your father is my godfather?'

'No!' The word came out as a gasp.

'And my father is Marco's godfather, and my mother godmother to Franco,' he said, referring to Elena's two el-dest brothers. His eyes were curious. 'Did you really not know this?'

She bit into her lip. 'It seems there's a lot I don't know.'

Gabriele stared closely, certain he could see tears brim-ming in her eyes. 'Are you feeling all right?'

She nodded then shook her head. 'Your mother...her mistaking me for *my* mother... That's the first time I've heard anyone refer to my mother as anything but an angel in heaven. In the Ricci world a woman is either a whore or a Madonna. To my father and my brothers, she's a Ma-donna without flaws *but she liked red wine*!'

A tear rolled down her cheek. She wiped it away.

'I didn't know she liked red wine. I knew our fathers were friends but I didn't know our families were such good friends too. We spent *Christmas* with you.'

Now it was his turn to take her hand and hold it tight. It felt cold. 'Our two families were like a real family from before even I was born, but everything changed when your mother died.'

'In what way?'

'It all stopped. When we first moved to America you and your family made plenty of visits. Your father was establishing his business here and I know your parents seriously considered emigrating too. But then your mother died and all the closeness was lost. All talk of emigrating stopped. Your father still visited us when he was in the country but the coming together of the two families…it just didn't happen anymore.'

'You visited us,' she said dully, shaking her head. 'I remember you and your dad staying at our house a couple of times. But that was so long ago.'

'Elena?' he asked when she drifted into silence.

She blinked. 'What you just said, I didn't know any of it.'

He reached out to finger a lock of her hair. 'Do you see why I loathe your father so much? We were family. I loved him. He didn't just set up my father, his oldest and closest friend, but he set up the man who had been like a brother to him. He let me, his own godson, go to prison. He knew my father had a heart condition but he didn't care. He let my father die.'

Her head shook slowly from side to side. 'He didn't,' she whispered. 'He wouldn't.'

'He did. And you *know* he did. You've seen for yourself the consequences of your father's actions—your father's betrayal, the shock of my imprisonment and the death of my father accelerated my mother's dementia.'

Quickly she wiped another fallen tear away and screwed her face, her lips trembling. Then she took an unsteady breath and sniffed lightly, swallowing as she visibly controlled herself.

'I'm sorry about your family and what you've all been through,' she said steadily, 'but I swear to you my family had nothing to do with it. My father is not that kind of man.'

She was lying. He could smell the lie falling from her tongue.

Was she lying to him or to herself? Because for the first time he truly considered whether Elena had been involved in her father's money-laundering racket and the cover-up that had led to Gabriele's father's door. Everything pointed to her having been purposefully kept aside by Ignazio.

But he knew better than anyone how Ignazio could form the most believable of trails.

'You said yourself that there were things about your life you didn't know; things your father and brothers kept from you. Is it not then conceivable that they would keep other things from you too?'

'No.' An obstinate look came on her face.

'Either you're in on it with them or you're in denial. Open your eyes. The truth is there waiting for you to find it.'

CHAPTER NINE

WAKING ALONE IN Gabriele's Florence home, a penthouse apartment spread over two floors overlooking Palazzo Tornabuoni, Elena wandered from the bedroom in search of coffee.

Even larger than his Manhattan apartment, it managed to be lavishly decorated and adorned yet remain homely. It had touched her to find he'd hung a Giuseppe Arcimboldo painting in the room he'd designated as her office.

Since their visit to his mother there had been a definite shift in their attitudes to each other. *Family* was a word no longer uttered between them. But it was constantly on Elena's mind.

How had her father been able to denounce Alfredo in such a way? And Gabriele, his own godson too. Why hadn't he helped their defence? *Of course* he hadn't been involved himself, but loyalty should have counted for something. Family loyalty was the crux of her father's personal philosophy and the Mantegnas *had* been family to him. She'd seen the photographic evidence with her own eyes.

And how could she not have known the full extent of their families' ties?

These were all questions she could not bring herself to ask him.

She had just settled on the balcony with a *caffe e latte* and fresh pastries made for her by Gabriele's housekeeper when he walked through the open French doors.

Her heart did that familiar little skip to see him.

'Good morning, *tesoro*,' he said, putting his hands on her shoulder as he leaned down to brush his lips against hers. 'You're up early.'

'Not as early as you.' She turned her cheek so he couldn't kiss her mouth.

In the ten days since they'd married her refusal to kiss him had become an unspoken rule. She would only allow him to kiss her when there were people around to witness it.

It was the only measure of control she had to hold on to. He never said anything to the contrary but she knew it got under his skin.

He hadn't been joking when he'd said they would spend the flight from New York getting to know each other better. Half an hour after take-off and they'd been locked in his jet's private bedroom. By the time they'd landed he'd made love to her so thoroughly and so often her legs had struggled to remain upright.

He'd kissed every part of her. He'd discovered erogenous zones on her body she hadn't known could *be* erogenous zones.

Every touch, every kiss, every murmur, every breath against her skin sent her senses into orbit and she had to fight to keep her responses contained.

As this was their so-called honeymoon period they spent nearly every waking minute together. They'd settled into a rhythm where the first hours of the day were spent working on issues for their respective businesses, then they would head out into Florence, or take a drive through the Tuscan hills. They'd visited museums, galleries and vineyards, eaten at a variety of restaurants and simple cafés, all the things Elena had never done before.

Growing up in the Ricci household, culture and days out were things people did on the television. Her father's idea of culture was a night out at the greyhound races.

While she and Gabriele didn't always agree on what made great art, often their views did concur. Arcimboldo wasn't the only artist they both admired.

She had to admit, she enjoyed his company. Their debates were always lively when they disagreed. He was opinionated and arrogant but he *listened* to her without the smug 'humouring you' look she was so used to seeing from her male family.

And they spent more time in bed than she had dreamed it was possible to spend. Only a fraction of that time was spent sleeping.

Gabriele was insatiable and, though she wouldn't give him the satisfaction of vocalising it, her desire for him was equally acute.

The only thing she wouldn't allow him to do in the privacy of their bedroom was kiss her on the mouth. That would be a betrayal to her family too far.

Because she had to remind herself frequently that the only reason she was there with him was to save her family. She was not with Gabriele for herself. Gabriele was her enemy and she would not allow herself to forget it, no matter how much she might enjoy his company or how much she secretly looked forward to going to bed with him every night.

Now he flashed her with a gleam of white teeth and helped himself to a banana.

'Have you been for a run?' she asked, taking in his workout attire. The apartment had a gym but neither of them had used it in the time she'd been there.

He nodded. 'I went down the Arno and up to Ponte Vecchio.'

'Sounds nice. When I'm at home in Rome I like to jog along the Tiber.'

'You're welcome to join me.'

An automatic refusal formed on her lips but she found herself saying, 'I might take you up on that.'

'I run every morning. Name your day.'

'I'll get back to you on that.'

He grinned. 'Don't worry—I'll slow down enough so you can keep up with me.'

'You don't think I can keep up with you?'

'You're half my size,' he pointed out, amusement lurking in his eyes, 'and I run every day. There's no question I'll have more stamina than you.'

If there was one thing Elena never backed away from it was a physical challenge. 'Tomorrow morning. What time do you want to leave?'

'I normally go as soon as I wake but I'm happy to wait until you get up.'

'No, no, you can wake me when you're ready.'

He fixed her with a wolfish grin and swallowed the last of his banana. 'It will be my pleasure to wake you up.'

Gabriele had known exactly what to say to get Elena out running with him. From everything she'd said about her childhood, the competition between her and her brothers had been fierce. Tell Elena she couldn't do something on account of being a woman and she would work twice as hard to prove she could.

It was a quality he admired.

He'd woken her at five, knowing to leave it much longer would mean losing the tranquillity of the early morning sunrise. While he loved Manhattan in the early hours, no city on earth could match Florence for beauty.

Apart from a tiny yelp when she'd seen the time, she'd thrown a pair of running shorts and a plain white T-shirt on without speaking. They'd set out at a gentle pace, jogging down Via degli Strozzi and on to Via della Vigna Nuova. Now, as they crossed Ponte alla Carraia, one of the bridges over the Arno River, she finally seemed to be waking up, continually scanning the skies to watch the sun make its first peeks.

'The best view to watch the sunrise is Piazzale Michelangelo,' he said.

'Can we go there now?'

'There isn't time—we'd need to leave at least an hour earlier than we did today.'

She made a noise under her breath that sounded remarkably like a curse.

'Early mornings not your thing?'

'Not that early.' Suddenly she turned to look at him, still keeping her stride. 'Have you been running every morning since we arrived here?'

'I told you, I run every day.'

'So you go for a run, get home and have a shower, all before I'm up?'

'Yes.'

'Are you a masochist?'

He laughed. 'The prison day starts early—I spent two years waking at four a.m. for the four-thirty cell-check. It became a habit.'

'That's barbaric,' she said with a shudder.

'You get used to it. Lights out was at ten-thirty so there was plenty of time to sleep.'

Elena fell silent, the only sound her breathing as she continued at the pace he'd set.

'How did you cope?' she finally asked.

'Prison?'

She nodded.

'I was fortunate that my lawyers were able to negotiate getting me into a minimum security prison so it could have been a lot worse. I won't lie; when I first walked through the doors I was sick with fear of the unknown but you adapt and it becomes…normal. But you know what kept me going?'

She didn't answer. Probably she knew what he was about to say.

'It was the thought of getting my revenge on your father. That's what got me through each day.

'But let's not spoil our time together on a subject we'll never agree on,' he continued, suddenly feeling like a heel for spoiling the peace that had settled between them. 'How are you finding the pace? Do you want to go slower? Faster? As we are?'

In reply, she accelerated, running ahead, her ponytail swishing behind her, her bottom swaying beautifully.

He laughed and increased his own pace to catch her. 'One day we'll have to have a proper race.'

'You'll beat me,' she said with certainty.

'That's not like you to be so defeatist.'

'It's called realism. I'm as fit as you are but you're more powerful. The only way I could beat you is if you were ill, which would make competing pointless.' She threw him a sly look. 'I'm certain I could beat you in a straight fight though.'

'I thought you were being realistic.'

'Wrestling and boxing were staples of our television viewing when I was a child. I copied their moves and used them on my brothers. They haven't beaten me in a one-on-one fight since I was eight.'

'You don't think they were going easy on you?'

'Not since the first time I beat them.' She flashed an evil grin. 'I wasn't averse to using pinches and scratches in sensitive places when it suited me. In that respect I had an advantage—my father would have killed them if they'd used the same tactics back at me.'

He grinned at the image. 'Didn't your father mind you fighting?'

'He thought it was funny to see his macho boys beaten by a girl. It's how I gained his respect.'

'You had to act like a boy to get it?'

By now they were crossing the Ponte Santa Trinita, back across to their side of the river.

'It was all of them,' she surprised him by saying. 'Not just my father. My earliest memories are of my brothers treating me like a doll. It *infuriated* me. My father thought it was funny to see his little girl pounding her fist into his youngest son's face. But it worked to his advantage.'

'How?'

'It gave him a legitimate reason to home educate me—

he couldn't send me to an all-girls private school if I was going to beat everyone up. My brothers went to school and had healthy social lives while I was kept locked away.

'Do you think I'm exaggerating?' she asked into his silence.

'No. I'd already guessed as much.'

'It was the excuse he needed. He wouldn't have let me go to school however I behaved. I was still a female and even though I had proven myself physically, I needed protection from the big wide world.'

'He wasn't disappointed his princess turned into such a tomboy?'

'Not in the slightest. There was no chance of me catching any boy's eye if I was dressed in filthy ripped jeans and exchanging punches with them every five minutes.'

Gabriele laughed but he didn't find it in the slightest bit funny.

'If he kept you hidden away so much, why did he let you join the company?'

'To keep me close and under his wing. My brothers and I always knew we would join the family company in one capacity or another and my father always knew he couldn't wrap me up in cotton wool once I'd come of age.' She stopped running and held a hand to her waist, kneading at a stitch with a pained face. 'He does love me, you know.'

'I know.'

'And he's changed a lot in his attitude towards me since I started working for him.'

'That's because he'd assumed you're immune to men seeing as you hadn't even had a boyfriend in twenty-five years,' Gabriele said astutely. 'Your father assumed his tomboy would be his princess for the rest of his life.'

'It's not like that.'

'Isn't it? Your mother died when you were a toddler. Your father closed ranks on all his children but especially with you. He kept you protected far beyond what any normal person would consider to be appropriate and all because you were a girl. If you'd been a boy your childhood would have been different and you knew it, so you became a boy to please him because you thought that's what he wanted.'

She shrugged, gave the side of her belly one last massage and set off again.

'Not quite. I saw that men were considered better than women and I would never be respected unless I made sure I never behaved like a girl. I didn't want to be a whore and I knew I could never be a Madonna so I became something entirely different that could never be interpreted as one or the other.'

'You do know that being a woman doesn't make you subhuman?' he said. He hated to think Elena had grown up believing that the only way she could have any respect was by being other than she was.

Did she even *know* who she was?

'Of course I know that.'

'Women are no more whores or Madonnas than men are misogynists or feminists. We all have our own capabilities and desires that are ours alone.'

She didn't answer, seemingly concentrating on the pathway ahead of them.

Now that the sun was up, the streets were getting busier with workers bustling to their places of employment, dog walkers and other early birds.

'We're nearly home,' he said, spotting a trattoria that was open for business. 'Let's get a coffee.'

They took a seat on an outside table and gave their order, both ordering a cappuccino and a chocolate pastry twist. The owner brought them a glass of water each with a, 'You look like you need it.'

Elena wiped her forehead with the back of her wrist. As far as Gabriele could tell, it was the only sign of perspiration on her, whereas his T-shirt was damp.

'How often do you see your father?' he asked conversationally. She'd spoken to him daily since their first morning in Florence when Ignazio had offered to fly his jet to Florence and rescue her.

She'd played her part beautifully, insisting she didn't need rescuing and that she was blissfully happy with her new husband.

When she'd hung up the phone, she'd looked at Gabriele and said, 'I really hate you.'

'I hope one day you understand that I'm not the monster you think I am,' had been his entire response.

Other than that, for a couple who considered each other criminals, they got along surprisingly well.

Now she said, 'I see my father about as much as you see your mother. I take care of Europe while he deals with Asia and South America with my brothers.'

'Who runs the North American division?'

'That's only a minor aspect of the business now. We sell components to car manufacturers there but our design and manufacturing teams are based in other countries.'

'They never used to be. When we emigrated your father created many divisions in the US. They've all been closed down and moved elsewhere—Brazil's his favoured place of business now.'

'And your point is?'

'How often does your father visit the US? When was the last time he set foot on US soil? When did any of your brothers last visit?'

'I don't know. I don't keep tabs on them.'

Their cappuccinos and pastries were brought out to them. As soon as they were alone again, Gabriele continued with the conversation.

'Does your father ever mention visiting the US?'

'No.' She swallowed a bite of her pastry and fixed narrowed eyes on him. 'What is it with all the questions?'

'Has it never occurred to you that there may be a reason your father doesn't visit the US any more?'

'No, and I would appreciate it if you would stop trying to poison my mind against him.'

'I don't want to poison your mind,' he said quietly. 'All I want to do is open it.'

Her green eyes suddenly fixed on him. 'Does this mean you believe that, whatever happened between our fathers, I had nothing to do with it?'

Her words resonated. 'Does this mean you accept that *I* was innocent?'

'I asked first.'

He took a long sip of his cappuccino, staring at the face that was becoming as familiar to him as his own.

'I don't know,' he answered heavily. 'It's inconceivable to me that you could not know of your father's criminality…'

She closed her eyes slowly, her shoulders slumping.

'But,' he continued, 'the more I get to know you, the harder I find it.'

'You have doubts?'

'Many of them.'

'I can't persuade you either way, can I?' she said sadly, then shook her head and looked back at him. 'I believe in *your* innocence.'

He found his throat closing, making a response hard. 'Why?'

'The more I get to know you, the more I know you wouldn't go on a vendetta for no good reason. You believe my father to be the guilty party and a part of you still thinks I'm involved too.' Her eyes were steady as she said, 'But it doesn't excuse what you've forced me to do. Nothing will ever excuse that. I might believe in your innocence but don't think for a minute that I forgive you because that will never happen.'

'I haven't asked for your forgiveness. If your innocence

is proven then I will apologise and hope for it,' he answered evenly. 'But let us not get carried away—you yourself admit the proof of your innocence doesn't exist.'

Elena stood under the hot stream of the shower and waited for the heavy pour to soothe her wounded heart. Until that morning, they'd both studiously avoided any conversation about her father or family in general and she wished she hadn't risen to the bait. She didn't want to spend their marriage at loggerheads and discussion simply opened raw wounds.

What she hated Gabriele for the most was the doubts he put in her mind.

The daily calls to her father had become excruciating. It didn't matter how often she told him everything was great, he didn't sound convinced.

What she hated hearing in his voice was the underlying panic. Because she couldn't trust it. She appreciated her marriage had been a shock to him but she definitely had the impression it was more than that; that her marriage to Gabriele scared him.

And try as she might to think otherwise, she couldn't help but wonder if he *had* been involved in Alfredo's fraud.

He wouldn't have set him up. She was certain of that. Not her father.

But what did she *really* know of his business dealings in South America and Asia? They were kept separate from the division she ran.

And Gabriele's question of when her father had last visited the US…

She truly couldn't remember. When she'd been a child he'd made regular trips there, often accompanied by one or other of her brothers, but she could not remember the last time any of them had mentioned a visit there for whatever reason.

Were they afraid to step foot on US soil? And if so, why?

Surely, she reasoned, if the US authorities suspected him of anything they could get an international arrest warrant?

But according to Gabriele, all the evidence was in the basement of the Nutmeg Island chapel, which the authorities couldn't touch without hard evidence.

How would her father react if she were to ask him for the chapel code…?

God, she loathed herself for doubting him. Hated that she had to bite back the question every time she spoke to him. Hated that she feared his answers.

And she hated that the images of those photos played so greatly in her mind.

There was a whole history between the two families that had been all but erased. All she'd ever seen of it was a blurred outline; all the colour and vitality within the outlines faded into darkness.

And she really hated that it made her wonder what else she'd been kept in the dark about.

CHAPTER TEN

MANTEGNA'S HEADQUARTERS WERE located on the outskirts of Florence, in a sprawling complex that covered two square miles of land set in a basin in the Tuscan hills. Elena's first glimpse was as they drove over the crest of a hill. There it lay beneath them, gleaming in the midday sun.

Gabriele had decided to drive, and he brought the small sports car to a stop so she could admire the view.

Dozens upon dozens of futuristic buildings and hangars were encircled by a testing track. In the centre of it all was the famous electric-blue main building itself, shaped in the diamond Mantegna logo with the silver M dashed across it, its roof shining and glossy under the sun.

Mantegna Cars had manufacturing plants the world over but here was its heart.

'Have the renovations finished now?' she asked.

When Gabriele had been halfway through his prison sentence, work had begun, to much fanfare, on expanding Mantegna's European headquarters to make them his worldwide HQ. It had been a defiant gesture that had told the world Gabriele would not be skulking away and his business would continue to thrive and innovate. Having been unaware of her own father's involvement—*supposed* involvement—in the fraud, believing her father to be an innocent bystander in the Mantegnas' criminality, she'd thought it showed a lack of class.

But you never thought your father was completely innocent, did you? That twisting you experienced in the pit of your belly whenever you heard details of the investigation and the trial were testament to that.

Coldness ran up her spine and she clasped her hands tightly together.

What kind of daughter was she to even consider her father being capable of such a thing?

'The bulk of it was completed a month ago,' he said, oblivious to her inner turmoil. 'We've had a few teething problems but nothing major. When we launch the Alfredo next month, everything will work perfectly.'

The supercar that would be a tribute to Gabriele's father and an event that had the world's motor press salivating with anticipation.

'How did you do it?' she asked in wonder. 'The boss of one of the world's greatest car manufacturers goes to prison for fraud and money laundering but instead of your business collapsing around you, it thrives and comes back stronger than ever.'

Gabriele stared out of the window as she spoke. It was a long time before he answered.

'It helped that my staff believed in me,' he said quietly. 'They carried the business during my incarceration. We were all determined to fight back and so were the majority of my financial backers. They believed in my innocence.'

He spread out his hands and nodded at the Mantegna building in the distance. 'The expansion sent out a message of intent to the world. The launch of the Alfredo will be the pinnacle; proof positive that our cars are the best in the world and that nothing will be allowed to destroy us.'

Elena stared at him with her heart in her mouth.

How did someone inspire such blind loyalty? She had no illusions about her own staff—their loyalty was to their pay cheques. All it had taken was a couple of unfounded whispers from Gabriele for a handful of her father's banks to call in their overdrafts.

Yet Gabriele's staff and backers had fought for him.

He set the car in motion again and soon they were walking into the foyer of the headquarters of Mantegna Cars.

The interior of the main building was as futuristic as the exterior, all glass walls and electric-blue furnishings.

Gabriele insisted on giving her a tour of the entire facility, introducing her to scores of people as they made their way through it all. Nothing was off-limits. All of Mantegna Cars' intellectual secrets were opened up to her in a display of trust she found astounding and also incredibly touching.

Since their jog together, they had found a relative harmony, but, with their wedding celebration party only a day away, her nerves were a tangled mess knowing her father and brothers would be attending.

This was the perfect way for her to forget what the next day would bring.

As Ricci Components made parts for cars, everything was familiar to Elena, and yet refreshingly different, as if she'd been beamed to the twenty-third century. There was little hierarchy either that she could discern, everyone treating each other with mutual respect. There was less of a gender divide than she'd expected too. In the main manufacturing plant there were a handful of women working who clearly weren't there for decoration or to make tea. It was a nice culture shock to have, especially as Ricci Components tended only to employ women for clerical roles.

She had come to accept that even her own job was clerical. Everything Ricci Components made was manufactured in Asia or South America. The closest she came to the manufacturing process was through imports.

'Your deputy Chief Engineer is a woman,' she commented with a shake of her head when they were walking back to the main building.

'Yes,' was Gabriele's reply, as if the matter were so inconsequential it didn't need discussing.

She wondered if the deputy Chief Engineer had had to fight misogyny to get where she was, both within her family and the world at large. Or had she a family that was supportive to all her dreams?

Back in the main building, Gabriele took her up to the media suite, where a group of executives was waiting for them, trays of food and coffee laid out.

A wall-length flat-screen television played a montage of the new Alfredo supercar driving through the Tuscan hills.

'It's stunning,' Elena marvelled as the screen changed to show the Alfredo powering up the German Autobahn.

'I'm pleased you like it,' he said with a grin.

'Is this the advert you'll be using?' she asked.

'This is only for the press launch. We don't need to advertise.' Gabriele took a bite of a mini cheesecake, noting the sparkle in Elena's eyes. She really was in her element here. 'We advertise heavily for our more family-oriented cars but our supercars are niche—only five hundred Alfredos will be manufactured and they're sold out already.'

'So why do any press for it?'

'This car is a tribute to my father. I want the world to see it. I want to remind the world of his innocence.' The dimming of her eyes made him feel like a heel. Wanting the light to come back into them, he added, 'The launch also gives publicity for the Mantegna name, and prestige for our buyers. They like belonging to an exclusive club that everyone knows about but can't join.'

Gratitude flashed in her eyes. 'I'm tempted to ask you to produce one more just for me.'

He laughed. 'A wedding present?'

'A divorce present,' she retorted drily.

He hooked an arm around her and kissed her temple. He liked that she didn't automatically freeze when he touched her now. He liked it a lot. 'I'll see what can be done.'

It was amazing, he reflected, that a month ago the thought of a Ricci—any Ricci—driving the car named after his father would have been a dagger through his heart.

'At the very least I can offer you a test drive,' he said. 'I'll arrange for Monty, our resident test driver, to take you out on the track next week.'

Her eyes widened with enthusiasm. 'That would be fantastic. Incredible.'

'Am I right in thinking Mrs Mantegna is a petrol head?'

'A what?'

'It's what they call car enthusiasts in the UK,' he laughed.

'I suppose I am.' She sounded surprised at her agreement.

'Many women are, you know. They don't have to pretend to be just to be accepted as one of the boys.'

'If that's the case, why don't you manufacture a supercar *for* women?'

'We do.' He grinned. 'You like the Alfredo, don't you? When you consider women have as much purchasing power as men, it's ludicrous not to cater for their tastes too. For the past decade we've made sure all our cars, from every range, have gadgets that appeal to women as well as those that traditionally appeal to men.'

She gave an approving, if puzzled, smile and he thought of her obvious surprise about his deputy Chief Engineer being a woman.

He looked more carefully at her. Today she was dressed in her usual uniform of slim-fitting dark trousers matched with a mauve blouse, her hair loose around her shoulders. She seemed to enjoy her new wardrobe but was still unsure about wearing make-up or doing anything with her hair other than a knot or ponytail.

For Elena, being a woman was something she had fought her entire life. A new wardrobe and one make-up lesson could not overturn a lifetime of learned behaviour, no matter how much she secretly wished it could. He'd seen her watch Internet videos on make-up tips and hairstyles, her face screwed in concentration, but she never attempted them herself. He was certain she did want to embrace her femininity but something held her back.

There were times he'd be watching her and he'd feel

such a heavy compression in his chest that his lungs would shrink and he would struggle to breathe.

It should be of no consequence to him whatever was going on in her head but it was there all the same. He wanted to scoop her thoughts out and throw away the ones that hurt her; the ones that told her she wasn't good enough as she was.

There were times he could almost understand why Ignazio had gone to such lengths to protect her. There was something about Elena that made a man discover his inner Neanderthal. She was such a strange mixture of vulnerability and fieriness; so capable and determined yet so fragile too.

He smiled ruefully. One thing Ignazio had failed to learn but had taken Gabriele all of five minutes in her company to discover was that Elena didn't need protection. She was more than capable of taking care of herself.

All she needed and all she wanted was respect.

Anna Maria came into the media room and caught his eye.

Excusing himself, he went to join her by the door.

There was an air of calm excitement about her.

'We've got the proof,' she said in an undertone.

Automatically, his gaze turned to Elena. She was now talking to the director of the promo that had been recorded.

'Are you certain?'

'Yes. Carlos came through. He's emailed the proof.'

Gabriele closed his eyes.

At last.

Carlos was one of Ignazio's closest aides. He'd worked with him for decades. Other than his children, there was no one Ignazio trusted more.

It had bitten at his craw to reach out to a man who had effectively betrayed his father as much as Ignazio had but desperate times called for desperate measures. He'd spent a lot of money buying Carlos's loyalty and now it appeared to be paying off.

'I need the originals.' He wanted the proof of his innocence to be cast iron. As he spoke, Elena turned her head, saw his eyes upon her, and gave a small, shy smile.

How would she react when she learned what he'd been doing behind her back?

How would she react when she learned he had the proof?

And how would she react when she discovered what he planned to do with it?

He hadn't lied to her. Their contract had been clear. Marriage and a baby in exchange for him destroying the documents he'd copied from the chapel basement.

Nowhere on the contract did it stipulate he couldn't continue digging for evidence to clear his father's name and have his own criminal record expunged.

That Elena had assumed this would be covered by the original verbal agreement was not his problem.

All the same…

His guts felt very heavy when he imagined what her reaction would be.

'How much did you miss having a mother when you were growing up?' Gabriele asked once they were driving back home.

He felt her eyes rest on him and knew she was reading his face before deciding whether to answer. They had learned to read each other well.

She was silent for a long while before replying. 'Not my childhood so much as my adolescence. That's when I really missed having her there.'

'No counterbalance for all the testosterone?' He changed gear and tapped the brake as they approached a small town.

She smiled faintly. 'None at all. I hardly ever met any women. I was home educated with male tutors—our household staff were all men too, as were all the cousins from my father's side.'

'What about the rest of your family? Did you ever see anyone from your mother's side? Aunts? Cousins?'

'My mother was Swedish and all her family live there. I saw them a handful of times when I was growing up.'

'And now? You spend a lot of time in Scandinavia working. That must make it easier to be in contact with them.'

'They're strangers to me. I was twelve the last time I saw any of them.'

'They don't have to be strangers any more.'

He felt green eyes upon him.

'I've got a couple of female cousins around my age who wanted to be friends but I snubbed them. It's too late for me to expect a relationship now.'

'Why did you snub them?'

A dry laugh. 'Because they were girls. And they were beautiful and poised and wore the most beautiful dresses, whereas I was a tomboy dressed for a party in boys' clothes.'

'Did you want to be like them?'

'I don't know.' She took a breath. 'I suppose I did want to be a little like them but I didn't know where to begin. And I didn't want to give my brothers any ammunition to remember *I* was a girl. Girls were cheap meat to be made fun of, remember?'

'I'm very sorry you grew up believing that.'

It was with a heavy heart that Gabriele locked his car and went into the apartment with Elena.

When she excused herself to take a shower, he took the opportunity to catch up on emails with some privacy.

Carlos had agreed to meet him in person. For an extra one hundred thousand dollars he would bring the originals with him.

Gabriele didn't quibble over it. He would spend any

amount of money to exonerate his father and clear his own name. Whatever it took.

Anna Maria was convinced that, for an even larger sum, Carlos could be persuaded to defect and testify in person. It would be Gabriele's job to persuade him.

The end game was coming. If he could convince Carlos to testify—and that was by no means a given—then Ignazio Ricci was finished.

But the gratification of a game plan coming to fruition was nowhere to be found.

When he and Elena went their separate ways she would be all alone. He knew her father's arrest would be painful for her; he couldn't bring himself to imagine *how* painful. Who would she turn to? Her brothers?

He almost laughed out loud at the thought of those idiots attempting to comfort her.

She had family in Sweden though…

He straightened, an idea formulating.

He put a quick call through to Anna Maria. 'I need you to track down Hilde Ricci's family in Sweden,' he said. 'Call me as soon as you have anything.'

Tomorrow night he and Elena would celebrate their wedding. *They* might know it was all for show but no one else did. He had a decent-sized family and numerous friends. The only people attending from her side were her father and brothers. If his idea paid off, he might be able to even it out a little for her.

Feeling moderately better in himself, Gabriele headed to the bedroom, certain she would have finished showering by now. Elena spent more time in the shower than anyone he'd ever known. With anyone else he'd see it as an invitation to join them but with Elena he knew it was her way of destressing away from him when her thoughts became too much.

She was bent over, a large towel wrapped around her, rubbing at her hair with a smaller one.

She spotted him, straightened, tightened the towel and scurried back into the bathroom.

After three weeks spending virtually every waking—and sleeping—moment together it was hard to believe she could still be so shy around him.

Inhaling deeply, he undressed.

Moments later she returned wearing her robe, the sash knotted so tightly he was surprised she could breathe.

Her eyes widened to see he'd stripped off to just his boxers.

'Are you going to shower now?' she asked, averting her gaze, colour creeping up her cheeks.

'Soon.'

When would she have the courage to be naked around him outside the bed itself?

'Are we still eating out?'

'Yes.' As neither of them could cook and it suited him not to have his housekeeping staff around too much—he'd noticed Elena was much less inhibited when it was just the two of them even if the needed privacy meant she wouldn't kiss him—they ate out most days.

Stepping over to her, he took her by the arms and gently swivelled her round to stand before the full-length mirror. He undid the knot of the robe, and smoothed the silk away from her shoulders, letting it pool at her feet.

'What do you see?' he asked.

She met his eyes in the reflection, a question in them. 'You and me?'

'Forget about me. Look at your reflection and tell me what you see.'

'I see…' she lifted a shoulder '…me.'

'And who are you?'

'Elena.'

'And who is Elena?'

Her lips clamped together.

Stepping behind her, he placed his hands to her jaw and

rubbed his fingers against her soft skin, then gathered her hair together and kissed the swan of her neck.

'When I look at you, I see a woman. A beautiful...' he kissed her shoulder '...intelligent...' he kissed the top of her spine '...passionate woman.'

Snaking his tongue down her back, he dropped to his knees and kissed her bottom.

'You are neither a whore nor a Madonna. You are a woman with desires and needs that are all your own.'

She stood still but he could feel little quivers emanating from her.

He inched himself around so her abdomen was level with his mouth. He placed his lips to it then looked up at her.

She was gazing down at him, her eyes apprehensive and confused but her colour raised.

'You are not a woman pretending to be a man, you *are* a woman. You have a spine of steel and a mouth tender enough to heal a wound with a kiss.'

He kissed into the dip of her side and trailed his tongue to her hip and zagged it slowly across to her pretty blonde mound.

Scenting her excitement, he pressed his nose into the fine hair and inhaled.

'You have the scent of a woman, not a man.' He flicked his tongue out and encircled her swollen nub.

A tiny moan came from her throat.

'You have the silkiest skin of *any* woman.'

Now her eyes were dark and hooded.

'Look in the mirror,' he whispered, 'and tell me what you see.'

She stared at herself.

'I see...' Her words were heavy, laboured.

'Do you see the woman with the power to be whoever she wants to be? Do you see the woman who can embrace the passionate core beating inside her? Because that's the woman I see when I look at you, Elena.'

Her hands reached down to take his head in her grasp, her fingers digging into his scalp.

Her desire, unspoken, was given as an invitation.

Burying his face in her heat and sliding a hand up her back to steady her, Gabriele gently used his tongue to bring her to the heights he knew gave her so much pleasure.

He doubted he would ever tire of watching her orgasm.

That first time had been special. Discovering her virginity in such a manner had been as much a shock to him as the feel of him inside her had shocked Elena. Watching that shock slowly turn into bliss and then wonderment, knowing it was his arms she was coming undone in... It had been more than special. He'd thought nothing would ever be able to match it.

Instead, his amazement had grown.

Though he knew his thoughts would only confirm Elena's opinion that all men were pigs, he couldn't help the delight it gave knowing only *he* had discovered Elena's hidden passion. Every response was his and his alone. And every time she touched him, it thrilled his selfish ego to know he was the only man she'd touched in this way. The only man she'd *ever* touched.

Her desire for him was not something she could hide—he had learned to read his wife very well. Her eyes responded in an honest way she still wouldn't allow her body to fully do.

He hoped the day would come when *she* seduced *him*. When she would press her lips to his and breathe into him.

If she would only let go, set all her inhibitions and doubts about him free and embrace with everything she had what could be explosive.

She had no reason to trust him. He knew that.

By the time he earned it, their marriage would be over. One way or another.

But then her fingers dug even harder into him and her

thighs trembled and his thoughts vanished, his concentration solely on her and her pleasure.

Only when he felt her go limp did he look back at her, smiling to see the dazed expression now echoing back at him.

Taking a firm hold of her hips, he got to his feet and lifted her into the air, a lock of her white-blonde hair falling into his face.

In three strides he carried her to the bed and laid her down.

She parted her legs for him and with one thrust he was inside her.

Until that moment he hadn't realised how deep his own ache had been.

It was an ache he carried with him on an almost permanent basis.

CHAPTER ELEVEN

IF ELENA'S NERVES got any tighter she would go springing across Piazza del Duomo.

Gabriele, who had earlier massaged her shoulders in an effort to relieve her tension, rubbed her wrist with his thumb.

'I'm sure your family will behave themselves,' he said. In the five-minute walk to the hotel they were throwing the party at, he'd made a variety of assurances at least seven times.

'It's not their behaviour that concerns me.' She was only half lying. Over one hundred people would be attending their 'celebration'. Every single one of them knew of the animosity between her father and her husband.

The media furore had died down in the past week, but today talk of their wedding celebration was everywhere. Rumours had circulated of paparazzi offering thousands of euros for an invitation. All anyone seemed to care about was who would hit who first—her husband or her father...?

Since when had she started thinking of Gabriele as her husband?

There was no time to ponder this strange turn of events as they'd arrived at the hotel.

A media scrum greeted them but the hotel had beefed up its security and cordoned the media away from the hotel steps.

Clinging tightly to his hand, she climbed the stairs under a hail of flashing bulbs and shouted questions.

Hotel staff greeted them in the foyer, welcoming them with glasses of champagne. Gabriele had booked the whole hotel, one of the oldest and most prestigious in Florence, for the evening, bedrooms and all.

Anna Maria was in the dance room waiting for them. Gabriele left them to it while he went to greet the band, infamous hell-raisers who'd had half a dozen global best-selling albums and who had flown in from America especially for the evening. While they milled by the free bar, their roadies were setting up on the stage.

'What do you think?' Anna Maria asked.

As Elena gazed around the room, taking it all in, she couldn't help the wistfulness that raced through her. The high vaulted ceiling and frescoed walls were magnificent on their own but the tables decorated with silver balloons and the scattering of tiny silver horseshoes, the streams of ribbon twisted around the pillars in the room's corners, gave it a romantic effect that made her ache that this was all a lie.

'It looks beautiful,' she said.

She looked over at Gabriele, deep in conversation with the band's singer, and wished...

Wished for what? That this could be real? That their marriage could be born out of love, not hatred and ven-geance?

He caught her eye and made a drinking motion, asking if he could get her anything.

Touched, she raised her still-full glass of champagne.

He winked and indicated he would be with her in a mo-ment.

Shaking off the wish that he were with her right now, she turned her attention back to Anna Maria, taking in the creased trouser suit she wore. 'Are you going to change soon?'

'I'm only here to oversee events,' the PA replied.

'That's what the hotel management's for,' Elena said. 'Take the evening off and join us.'

'I can't.'

Rooting through her small clutch bag, Elena found her credit card. 'There's a boutique and a hairdresser here in the hotel. Take this and buy yourself something. I'm sure the hotel will have a room you can get ready in.'

Anna Maria shook her head, now looking ill at ease. 'I truly can't.'

'You can. I insist. I'll clear it with Gabriele for you.'

At the mention of his name, something flickered on Anna Maria's face.

For the briefest moment Elena wondered if the PA was in love with him but immediately discounted the idea. She wasn't an expert on relationships but not once had she felt any vibes that suggested they were anything but boss and employee.

Maybe the PA disapproved of their farce of a marriage and didn't think it appropriate to join in with the mock celebrations?

'Please,' she said, touching her hand and deciding to change tack. 'We both know the truth about my marriage, there's no need to pretend otherwise, but that doesn't mean you can't enjoy the evening. I won't know many people here and it will be nice to have a familiar face in the crowd.'

Anna Maria bit into her lip. When she looked at Elena there was something in her expression that set off a fresh warning of something being wrong. But then she smiled and nodded her head.

'Thank you. That's very kind of you.'

'Go and make yourself look beautiful.'

Anna Maria spoke briefly to Gabriele, who sent Elena another wink, then she disappeared from the room.

Elena continued gazing at him, happy to observe from afar. He looked gorgeous in his black tuxedo and bow tie, a powerhouse of masculinity that perfectly complemented the femininity she could feel racing through her blood.

Tonight she truly felt like a woman.

Of all the dresses she'd bought on Liana the stylist's recommendation, this was the one she'd never had any intention of wearing. For a start, it showed off flesh. *Her* flesh. Made of silk crepe de Chine that felt heavenly against her skin, the spaghetti straps and low-cut front skimmed both sides of her breasts, making the wearing of a bra impossible. Monochrome swirl prints interspersed with turquoise fell in layers, one side to mid-thigh, the other to mid-calf, and swayed when she walked. And speaking of walking...

She'd squeezed her feet into a pair of blush-coloured five-inch-high sandals with one simple strap across her toes that was nonetheless crystal embellished, and a thin ankle strap. She'd never felt so tall. Her legs had never felt so shapely.

A visit to a salon had seen her hair swept into a loose but elegant chignon, her fringe swept to one side and tendrils left loose around her ears and her nape. She'd kept her make-up simple but after weeks of determined practice she was finally getting the hang of it.

As vain and silly as she knew it to be, she now loved wearing make-up and felt nothing but sadness that she had spent so many years denying this side of her nature, not just denying it but pretending it didn't exist.

Gabriele had taken one look at her and wolf-whistled.

That man...how could the one person she should hate more than any other on the planet be the one to make her look in a mirror and find the real woman beneath the skin?

With a start she realised she didn't hate him any more. And when he came over and took her hand in his, she squeezed it, her heart so full, her chest so tight she couldn't speak.

'That was a lovely thing you did for Anna Maria,' he said quietly, handing her credit card back to her. 'I've told her to put whatever she buys on the account. I should have thought of it myself.'

The temptation to reach out and touch his face was strong but some last resistance lay within her and she slipped the card back into her bag, saying, 'She looked so tired I almost ordered her home.'

He gazed into her eyes as if he were searching for something.

The urge to touch him grew and she raised her chin towards his, parting her lips…

A loud noise from the stage broke the moment and she quickly looked away, trying desperately to regain control of herself.

'The guests are arriving,' she murmured, glad of the distraction, horrified that she had been about to kiss him, not for show but because at that moment she had wanted nothing more than to feel his mouth upon hers.

Soon the dance room was filled with guests, all of whom had to congratulate the happy couple. Even though they'd put on the invitations that the only present they required was their guests' company, many came with gifts, which Elena felt terrible about accepting. She kept staring at the table laden down with beautifully wrapped packages with that same tugging wistfulness in her belly she had felt when she'd walked into the room; that sensation of wishing that this could really be…

She knew from Gabriele's body language when her family arrived.

They were talking to a couple whose names she couldn't remember when he stiffened and his hold on her hand tightened.

'Elena's family are here,' he said politely. 'We need to go and welcome them.'

Her heart pounding so loudly it muffled her hearing, she walked with him to the bar, where her father and brothers were standing, champagne flutes in hand, although she would bet that any moment they would be ordering double Scotches.

The four Ricci men stood in a row facing them.

It was like a Mexican stand-off and, judging by the

looks in their eyes, they were all waiting for her to decide which side she was on.

How could she tell them that there was no choice and that if she didn't stay on her side of the invisible dividing line, they would likely all go to prison?

You don't know if you even want to return to their side of the divide.

Fixing a smile to her face, she embraced them in turn, wishing so hard she didn't feel like such a traitor, not just by her actions but by her emotions too. She had as little control over the latter as she had the former.

'Thank you so much for coming,' she said brightly, then stood back as Gabriele extended his hand to her father, forcing Ignazio to shake it.

She winced. She didn't know who tried the hardest to crush the other but any moment she expected to hear the sound of snapping bone.

When Gabriele shook her brothers' hands, it was their turn to wince.

After the 'niceties' had been observed, Roberto, the youngest of her brothers, looked her up and down, a smirk on his face. 'What's Mantegna done to you? You look like a girl.'

'More like a whore,' Franco muttered under his breath, yet audible enough for Elena to hear.

Her whole body flushed at the insult she had spent her entire life trying to avoid being on the receiving end of.

Before she could think of a suitable response—her brothers' guffaws only added to the brain-melting humiliation—Gabriele fixed them all with a stare that stopped their laughter in its tracks.

He took her hand in his and held it possessively.

'Your sister is a beautiful, intelligent woman,' he said, undisguised contempt in his voice, 'and I would appreciate it if you kept any sexist digs you may have in mind out of her earshot and definitely out of mine.'

All four Ricci men gaped at him, then identical fury flashed over their features.

Her father elbowed Franco, a silent but painful warning to keep his mouth shut.

The problem for her father and brothers was that they knew Gabriele had an agenda in marrying her but they didn't know what it was or how he intended for it to work out. They couldn't afford to antagonise him any further.

'Excuse us, but some new guests have arrived.' Gabriele's tone was like ice but his smile did not falter. 'I'm sure we'll have a chance to catch up later. The buffet will open soon so you'll have much to occupy you.'

When he bore her away, Elena didn't know whether to shout at him for his subtle rudeness or laugh at the memory of her brothers' gawping faces.

What she really didn't want to do at that moment, though, was shed the tears clamouring behind her eyes.

For the first time in her life she had looked at her immediate family and *really* seen them. She had seen four squat, overweight men who looked as if they were auditioning for the role of petty gangsters in a Scorsese film.

And then Gabriele introduced her to someone who made all thoughts of her father and brothers take a back seat.

'Elena?' said the elegant blonde woman before her.

'Aunt Agnes?' So shocked was she that she could hardly get the words out. She didn't have to say anything else for Agnes yanked her into her arms for a tight embrace.

'It is so good to see you,' Agnes said in perfect Italian. 'I have missed you terribly.'

By the time her mother's sister let her go, the threatening tears had spilled out.

'Are you here alone?' Elena asked after she'd blown her nose on a tissue Gabriele had thrust into her hands before he'd kissed her neck and whispered that he would leave them to it.

'Henrick is in Canada on business but Lisbeth travelled

with me—she's just changing Annika's clothes. Did you know she had a baby?'

Elena shook her head.

'Malin wanted to come too but she's due to give birth in three weeks herself so she wasn't allowed to fly, but she sends her love. Is your father here?'

'Yes.'

Agnes grimaced but didn't elaborate on her thoughts. Before Elena could ask, Agnes waved over Elena's shoulder. 'There's Lisbeth and baby Annika now.'

More embraces were shared and then they found a table to sit around and catch up on. Baby Annika was handed to her and Elena gazed down at the chubby little face with awe.

'I can't believe you've had a baby,' she said in wonderment. 'The last time I saw you, you were still in a training bra.'

Lisbeth laughed. 'The last time I saw you, you called me a silly girl and pulled my hair.'

Elena winced.

Lisbeth took her hand. 'I forgive you,' she said, so earnestly Elena smothered a laugh.

'I feel so bad that I haven't kept in touch,' she confessed a short while later.

'That wasn't your fault,' Agnes interjected. 'I take responsibility for that. I never should have suggested to your father that you come and live with us.'

'Did you?' Something else she hadn't known.

'When you were twelve. You were so unhappy and I—rightly or wrongly—thought it unfair of your father to lock you away as he did. I thought he would be happy for you to have some female guidance but he thought…otherwise.'

'Is that why we stopped seeing you?' They had never seen a huge amount of her mother's family, just the odd family party here and there, but it had stopped completely around the time of Elena's early adolescence.

'You know what your father's like. He rules with an iron fist and does not appreciate dissent, especially from a woman.'

Elena gazed at Gabriele, standing with a crowd of men, all of them roaring with laughter.

Gabriele would never treat a woman as anything but an equal. And he would never lock a child away. He might have stipulated that no child they had be allowed anywhere near her father or brothers but once a child came he would change his mind if he could see it would be in the child's best interests.

She kissed baby Annika's sweet scented head.

A pang rippled through her to think of the child she and Gabriele would have together.

There might be a little cluster of cells in her that very second, steadily forming into an embryo that would be part her and part Gabriele.

He had done this for her. He had brought her family over from Sweden without her knowledge. He'd given her back the family she hadn't known how much she needed.

It was the best present she had ever had.

Agnes followed her gaze. A smile tugged at her lips. 'I think your husband could not be less like your father. He must love you very much.'

No. He didn't love her. Gabriele could never love someone with Ricci blood. But what he'd done in bringing her family to Italy…

But of course this went unsaid. Elena forced a smile to her face and took a sip of champagne.

A few minutes later he was at their table.

'Excuse me, ladies, but I need to borrow my wife. It's time for us to say a few words to our guests.'

Taking his hand, Elena got up, promising to continue their talk later.

'Can you give me a minute to use the bathroom?' she said, wanting some time to compose herself and fix her face.

'Of course.' He rubbed a finger up her cheekbone and smiled, his eyes flashing. 'You really do look incredibly beautiful. You *are* incredibly beautiful.'

She wanted to thank him, not just for the compliment, which she truly believed he meant, but for what he'd done in bringing her family here. But her throat had closed and she couldn't get the words out.

'I'll wait for you by the bar,' he said before placing the softest of kisses to her lips.

Diving into the ladies', she went straight to the mirror and took a deep breath.

What was happening to her? Her emotions were all over the place, pulling her in directions she knew could never lead anywhere.

Was she suffering from a version of Stockholm syndrome? She'd heard of kidnapped women falling for their captors and making excuses for them but had never understood how such a thing could happen.

But she *hadn't* fallen for Gabriele, she told herself stubbornly. She'd just come to accept he wasn't the complete bastard she had thought him to be. He was much more complex than that.

And so were her emotions.

Satisfied her face was repaired as well as it could be, she left the sanctuary of the ladies' to find her father waiting for her.

He opened his arms and she gratefully slipped into his embrace.

How could she have such doubts about him? He was her father. He'd raised her alone and while he had certainly made mistakes he'd only ever done his best by her.

Hadn't he?

'You are happy, Elena?' he asked, stepping back a little but keeping a tight hold on her arms to peer at her closely.

What was he looking for? Signs of her doubt?

The disloyal thought made her feel even worse.

'Mantegna, he treats you well?'

'He treats me very well and I'm very happy with him.'
And as she spoke the words she knew them to be true.

She *was* happy with Gabriele.

There were times—many times—when she forgot why
she was with him and would feel full to the brim. And he
treated her better than she had ever been treated in her
life. He listened to her. He took her opinions as seriously
as he took his own. He made love to her as if she meant
something to him.

If he could treat her, a Ricci, like that, she could only
imagine how he would treat a woman he was in love with.

His ex-fiancée needed her head examined. If she'd been
Sophia she would have fought to clear his name. She would
never have doubted him.

Her head began to swim.

'When are you coming back to work?' her father asked,
still holding her arms. 'Your staff miss you.'

'I need to sort some things out,' she said, avoiding a
straight answer. Because what her father hadn't mentioned
was that she hadn't stopped working. She might not have
physically gone to work since marrying Gabriele but she
communicated with her staff daily and dealt with any problems as and when they occurred. Which was rarely. 'I'm
sure I'll be back in the office soon.'

*Back in the office, running myself ragged around Eu-
rope, trying desperately to justify why I have the position
I worked so hard for but which is ultimately worthless.*

These weeks away had forced her to see the truth. Her
job was nothing but a sop. She was nothing but a highly
paid supervisor. The divisions she managed didn't need
her. They were well run by their individual management
teams and functioned perfectly well without her.

She didn't even enjoy it!

Why had it taken her so long to see the truth?

But what else could she do?

She wasn't qualified to do anything else.

'I'll let you know very soon,' she promised, kissing his cheek and gently extracting her arms from his hold.

'If he hurts you…'

'I know.' She nodded wryly. 'I'll tell you. But he won't hurt me.'

'What does he say about me?' he asked as she made to move away.

She had dreaded this question, had been certain that when confronted with it the temptation to confess all would be too great, that she wouldn't be able to lie to him.

It was the look in his eyes that made her keep her confessions to herself.

He was worried about something.

And it *terrified* her to think what that something could be.

She was saved from having to answer by the singer of the band doing a call-out for her from his vantage point on the stage. Gabriele was standing by the stage, his arms folded and a mock-scowl on his face.

She gave her father one last impulsive hug, cleared the lump in her throat, and made her way through the laughing crowd to the stage.

Gabriele watched his wife walk to him, so much flittering over her face he couldn't discern one distinct emotion. Until she looked at him that was, and all her features softened and something flickered in her eyes he'd never seen before.

He didn't think he'd ever seen a more beautiful woman than Elena that night. When she finally reached him and took his hand, a tightness pooled in his gut that almost doubled him over.

The singer from the band said a few words then handed the microphone to Gabriele, who jumped straight into his thanks to everyone for attending and apologised for marrying in such haste.

'You know what it's like,' he drawled, pitching his speech between humour and sincerity, 'you meet someone and within a day the life you know is gone and you find yourself signing the *rest* of your life away.'

He waited for the laughter to subside before continuing. 'But that's what love does to you. It turns everything on its head and marks you to the person you've fallen for.'

His intention had been to direct those last words at Ignazio, to hammer home the message that Ignazio's beloved daughter had got into bed with the enemy, but he couldn't do it. He couldn't tear his gaze away from the woman who wore his ring.

He thought of Ignazio's right-hand man, who was on the brink of defecting to him with all the incriminating documents. He thought of how Elena would react when she learned of this and learned that he still intended for her father to spend the rest of his miserable life in prison.

But then he thought of his own father, dying within days of Gabriele being incarcerated, knowing full well that his only son was innocent and the man he'd considered a brother had betrayed him in the most heinous way.

He thought of his mother, so full of life if a little forgetful when this nightmare had started, the stress of seeing her son imprisoned and the sudden death of her husband accelerating the loss of her mental capacity at an alarming rate.

That was all Ignazio's doing.

It came to him that he hadn't added Sophia to that list.

But then Sophia paled in comparison to Elena. Elena would never have abandoned him. She would have been one of those wives who visited every weekend, the first to arrive and the last to leave. She would have believed in his innocence.

She *did* believe in his innocence. After everything he was doing to her, she believed him.

If he took the proof to the FBI as he intended then she would never believe in him again.

It would devastate her.

Could he really do that to her?

Hadn't she suffered enough?

The cheers from their guests brought him back to the present.

His silence had been so long they clearly assumed he'd finished. He couldn't remember the rest of what he was going to say anyway.

The band started playing again.

'Shall we dance?' he said.

Her hand was still in his. She gave one of those shy smiles he adored so much and nodded.

He led her to the centre of the dance floor and took her into his arms.

Smiling, she looped her arms around his neck and sighed, gazing up at him. 'Thank you for bringing my family here.'

He knew she didn't mean the Mantegnas.

'You're welcome. They seem like nice people.'

'They do.' Her eyes shone. 'Thank you.'

She moved closer to him, their legs touching, his groin pressing into her abdomen, even with the height of her sandals giving her an extra lift. And then she raised herself onto her toes and, her eyes still gazing into his, pressed her mouth tentatively to his.

He stilled, unsure whether this was a kiss of gratitude or something more.

Only when she tightened her hold around his neck and parted her lips did he dare believe it was something more.

Her sweet breath suffused him. Her sweet scent filled him. The softness of her lips…

He forgot that only weeks ago this party had been arranged with the sole purpose of showing Elena off on his arm in front of her father and letting him know in no uncertain terms that she belonged to him.

None of that mattered.

Elena was kissing him with feather-light movements and the tiniest darts of her tongue, and it was the most erotic, moving kiss he had ever experienced.

Running his hand up her spine, he captured the nape of her slender neck and kissed her back with the same languidness she kissed him.

When she eventually broke away, she buried her head in his shoulder and gave a muffled laugh.

He squeezed her tightly, adoring the feel of her pressed so close to him. And wished that everything could be different.

CHAPTER TWELVE

THE REST OF the evening passed in a happy daze. Elena had never expected to enjoy the party but she did. Meeting her Swedish family had been the pinnacle and when she and Gabriele left it was with promises to visit them very soon.

They took the short walk back to the apartment in silence, hands clasped, tension thick between them. Gabriele had long since removed his dinner jacket and bow tie, but the night air was so warm he slung it over his shoulder rather than put it back on. Or was it the heat swirling between them keeping him warm?

She had never felt such *depth* for someone, or such gratitude. Every time she remembered her brothers' faces when he'd reprimanded them she wanted to laugh. Every time she thought of what he'd done in bringing her Swedish family there she wanted to cry. It had been the most thoughtful thing she could imagine and he'd done it without any selfish motive. He'd done it for *her*.

She could never explain how much it meant.

The only way she'd been able to think to show how much it meant was by giving him the one thing she'd been denying him. She'd kissed him.

And now she knew it hadn't just been him she'd been denying by her refusal to kiss but herself too.

In the apartment they went straight to the bedroom, Gabriele throwing his dinner jacket onto a chair as they passed.

Elena closed the door behind them and leant against it, tugging at the ankle straps of her sandals and kicking them off, staring at *him*, the most beautiful man in the world.

And he stared right back, a fever in his eyes that filled every crevice.

She held out a hand. When he reached to take it, she took a step towards him and placed his palm on her chest, letting him feel the hammering of her heart. Her lonely heart that had somehow, without her knowing when or how, become whole.

His breathing was as heavy as her own, his eyes dark, molten.

Stepping even closer, she placed a kiss on his neck and inhaled his scent, then slowly moved her lips up, over his jawline, across his cheeks and then to his mouth.

She breathed him in as she kissed him and wound her arms around his neck, exploring him with her lips and her tongue, heat filling her trembling body.

He held her securely to him, letting her take the lead.

Dragging her fingers down his chest, she undid the buttons on his shirt, their kisses deepening.

One hand still splayed on the base of her back, he undid his trousers. Between them they removed his shirt and tugged his trousers and underwear down until he stood naked, his erection jutting against her belly.

She'd never known she could feel such need for someone. She'd never dreamt there would come a day when she would physically ache for a man and that her heart would race so hard it would feel bruised.

Now she broke the kiss and took a step back.

Gabriele thought he might be drowning.

He'd never known one kiss could make his entire body ignite with something more combustible than mere lust.

Whatever this was, he'd never felt it before. There was a voice in his head warning him of danger but he was helpless to obey it.

He didn't want to obey it.

Right now, this moment, Elena kissing him as if she

would consume him, every one of her looks spearing him…
it would be easier to slice a limb off than walk away.

'Get on the bed,' she whispered, standing as still as a
statue, only the rise and fall of her chest showing life…and
those mesmeric eyes that bore into him.

On legs that felt strangely boneless, he did as she bid,
not taking his eyes off her.

Only when he was leaning back against the headboard
on the bed did she come back to life.

She took a deep, trembling breath then gathered her
dress in her hands and pulled it up and over her head. The
movement dislodged whatever had been holding her hair
in place, white-blonde locks spilling over her shoulders.

All she had on now was a pair of lacy white panties.

She gazed at him, colour on her face, but made no attempt to cover herself as she usually did.

He swallowed the moisture in his mouth, gripping hold
of the bed sheets lest he jumped out, threw her onto the
bed and plunged inside her as the aching jut between his
legs longed to do.

She walked to him, not taking her gaze from him, until
she stood at the edge of the bed and slowly, *torturously*
slowly, tugged her panties down.

Climbing onto the bed, she straddled him, then her hot,
sweet mouth was back on his and she was kissing him as
if she needed his breath for life.

And then that beautiful mouth was dragging down his
throat, her tongue darting out, and she was kissing him everywhere, moving down his chest, his abdomen, her fingers exploring, so many sensations igniting that it was a
struggle to breathe.

When she took him into her mouth his hands clenched
into fists and he had to force air into his lungs.

He'd never experienced anything like it, such pure, deep
desire. It burned him.

Groaning, he watched her head bob up and down, desperate to reach out and touch her but not wanting to do anything that might scare her or break her from the moment.

Just at the point when he felt he might burst, she trailed her tongue back up his chest, her breasts brushing against his skin, until she found his lips. At the same moment her tongue swept back into his mouth, she sank down on him, taking him inside her sweet tightness in one long movement.

He watched her eyes close and a look of bliss spread over her beautiful face.

Wrapping his arms around her, he held her tightly, fusing her to him as she began to move, little cries escaping from her mouth that soon turned into moans and then gasps.

For so many nights he'd dreamed of her submitting to the desire gluing them together and letting herself go.

He'd never imagined it would be like this or dreamt it would *feel* like this.

He didn't want it to end.

When he felt his orgasm welling up inside him, he gritted his teeth to hold on, but the softness of her skin against him, the feel of being so perfectly fitted inside her, the friction of her movements, her breath and scent filling his senses…it was a battle he was about to lose.

And then she was crying out his name and sinking as hard onto him as she could, thickening around him, somehow pulling him even deeper into her.

He let go.

'Elena, God, Elena,' he breathed with the last of his air, white light flickering behind his eyes and pulsations ravaging him, taking him to a place he had never known existed.

His heart had never beaten so fast.

Much later, when lethargy had crept through his bones and sleep arrived to claim him, Elena entangled in his arms and breathing rhythmically, he opened his eyes for one last look at her and pressed the lightest of kisses to her forehead. Then he fell into the deepest, most content sleep of his life.

* * *

Gabriele gave his morning run a miss. Or, rather, his morning run gave *him* a miss. Today the sun had beaten him awake. And so had Elena.

He found her on the balcony, drinking coffee and gazing out at waking-up Florence.

Her face lit up with a smile to see him.

They'd shared a bed for almost three weeks yet this morning it felt as if he were handling the morning-after for the very first time.

He wanted to scoop her up and carry her back to bed.

Conversely, he wanted to get his training shoes on and run away as fast as he could.

He settled on taking a seat next to her and pouring himself a coffee.

'I hope you don't mind me wearing this,' she said shyly, indicating his navy robe, which she had wrapped herself in.

Seeing her dwarfed in *his* robe, her hair mussed from a night of lovemaking, a sparkle in her eyes…

His chest constricted, the palms of his hands dampening.

'Not at all.' He added a splash of milk to his cup. 'You're up early.'

The sparkle faded a little and she took a sip of her coffee. 'I woke up with cramps.'

'Are you okay?' he asked, immediately concerned.

'I've taken some painkillers. But it does mean I'm not pregnant.'

Relief surged through him in a whoosh.

He hadn't even realised this was news he'd been hoping for.

Elena wasn't pregnant. He got to keep her for longer.

He stared at her, trying to read her expression. 'You're disappointed?'

Was she really that keen for them to be over? When she conceived their child she could walk away.

But surely she didn't want to walk away after the night they'd just shared?

She would walk away if she learned what you were up to.

'A little.' She took another sip. 'I don't know why I thought it would happen so quickly.'

'It will happen when it's ready.' He ran a thumb against her cheek, thrilling when she rubbed into his touch. He adored her cheekbones; they were made for touching. 'You really do want to have a baby?'

He should have asked her before. Before he made her sign a contract where her only means of escaping him was by carrying his child.

What had he been *thinking*?

What kind of monster had he become?

And what could he do about it?

Her eyes were wide as she nodded. 'Very much. I never thought I would...'

'Because only girls have babies and you didn't want to be a girl?' he supplied.

She laughed, visibly relaxing. 'That was certainly a part of it. But don't forget I'd intended to stay a virgin until I died and seeing as a man's help is needed in making a baby...' She laughed again. 'I just never thought I would be in the position where a baby could be possible.'

She made it sound as if he'd given her a choice in the matter when the choice he'd presented her with had been no choice at all.

How could she even exchange a civil word with him?

Her hand crept onto his and squeezed. 'You need to get going soon, don't you?'

'Yes.'

He didn't want to leave her.

He couldn't wait to get away.

What was happening to him?

'I'll be back Tuesday,' he said, getting to his feet then leaning over to capture her lips.

He'd told her yesterday morning that he needed to go to America on business. He hadn't specified which American continent and she hadn't asked. She had no idea he was travelling to Brazil.

It would be the first time they'd been parted since he'd rescued her from those thugs on Nutmeg Island.

Her arm looped around his neck and she kissed him back, her teeth razing gently along his bottom lips when she pulled away, still holding him, and gazed into his eyes.

'When you get home…' She swallowed, colour flooding her cheeks. 'We can enjoy trying again to make a baby.'

How could she be like this around him? How could she even bear to look at him?

He took a deep breath and gave her one final, lingering kiss.

He prayed it wouldn't be their last.

As he got into his waiting car an hour later, he knew he would have to come to a decision soon. Tomorrow he would meet Carlos in Brazil. If Gabriele played his cards right, the original documents would be handed over. If he could meet Carlos's price, he should be able to persuade him to testify in person.

If everything went as he hoped, Ignazio would be arrested within days.

And he would lose Elena.

Elena got out of the test car and pulled the helmet off her head, unable to wipe the beam from her face.

That had to count as one of the best experiences of her life.

Monty, the official test driver, had called her that morning to say he had an unexpected free window and the test car was available for her to take out on the track. She hadn't needed asking twice. She'd jumped straight into the small Mantegna sports car Gabriele had given her the keys to before he'd left, and only just kept within the speed limit in her rush to Mantegna HQ.

Monty had driven the first couple of laps, explaining all the pertinent information before letting her loose. After a cautious first lap, she had put her foot down, the speedometer reaching one hundred and ten miles an hour before she'd lost her nerve and slowed it to a more reasonable ninety.

It had been an amazing experience.

What had made it extra special was knowing she had enjoyed it for herself; not as a means of proving a point to the men of the world—specifically her father and brothers—but for the sheer exhilaration.

Finally she understood what Gabriele meant about her having desires that were specific to *her* and not her gender. She was a woman learning to embrace the feminine side of her nature but also learning that the feminine side didn't exclude the traditionally masculine pursuits she enjoyed.

She suspected she would have enjoyed punching her brothers when she'd been a child even if she'd been dressed in pretty pink dresses and had her hair tied in neat little plaits.

Gabriele had done this for her. He'd opened her eyes and forced her to see and accept who she really was: a flesh and blood woman.

Knowing he was mid-air, flying back to Florence, she hadn't bothered calling to tell him she would be testing the car. He'd told her to expect him home late afternoon so she would tell him about it then. And tell him she'd decided to resign from her job. That was something that had solidified in her mind over the past couple of days, when Gabriele's absence had given her time to really think.

She'd missed him so much it scared her. It was like a great hollow ache in her entire being.

She knew the day would soon come when she would have to live with missing him permanently. They had no future. They never would.

However her feelings had developed, she still had Ricci blood running through her veins.

But something *had* passed between them the night of their party; changed them fundamentally. Whether it was enough…

Enough for what though? For a life together? A real life?

After Monty had put the boiler outfits they'd been wearing away, they headed back to the car park.

About to walk through the double doors, Elena did a double take at a car parked at the front and the driver leaning against its door smoking a cigarette.

'Is Gabriele here?' she asked the receptionist when she'd got inside the main building.

'He arrived an hour ago,' the receptionist said, recognising her. 'He's in his office.'

'Thanks.' Checking her phone for any missed calls or messages, of which there were none from Gabriele, she climbed the stairs.

What was he doing here? When she'd spoken to him last night he hadn't mentioned anything about coming back early.

Excited to see him, Elena hurried her pace, heading in the direction she recalled his office being in.

Taking a left at the top of the stairs on the third floor, she passed a skinny man in a garish silver suit. Thinking he looked familiar but unable to place where from, she arrived at Gabriele's office door.

She knocked, not wanting to presume too much and barge in without invitation.

The door was opened by Anna Maria, whose eyes widened to see her.

From behind the desk, visible from her vantage point at the threshold, Gabriele shot to his feet.

'Elena? What are you doing here?' he asked hoarsely.

They were both clearly shocked to see her. No, make

that horrified. They looked like a couple of children caught in the act of stealing.

Anna Maria appeared frozen, making no attempt to get out of her way. Elena pushed past her and strode to the desk.

'What's going on?' she demanded, half expecting to see discarded underwear on the floor.

'Nothing.' A sheath of papers was strewn over the desk, which he was gathering together. 'I wasn't expecting you.'

'I've been on the test drive you suggested Monty take me on.' As she spoke, she tried to see what was on the papers. Whatever they were, Gabriele didn't want her to see them, not if the way he was rushing to file them away was anything to judge by.

Something icy cold snaked up her spine.

That man in the corridor…

She snatched the papers from Gabriele's hand.

'Elena—'

He tried to take them back but it was too late.

She only needed a quick scan for her eyes to swim and her brain to fill with cold fog.

That man. *She knew who he was.*

'No,' she whispered, shaking her head violently. 'No.'

Discarded underwear would have been preferable to this.

Not taking her eyes from Gabriele's white face, she said, 'Anna Maria, leave us.'

The door slammed sharply.

'I suppose this explains why Anna Maria has been so uneasy around me,' she said in a voice that sounded distant to her ears. 'She's known from the beginning?'

Gabriele dropped the papers onto the desk and stared at her with black ringing eyes. 'Elena, let me explain.'

The coldness cleared, replaced with red-hot fury that she controlled by a whisker.

'What do you want to explain? How you've been lying to me all this time? How you tricked me into marrying you to save my father from a prison sentence when all the time you were still plotting against him?'

Of all the things she'd struggled to believe since that fateful night on Nutmeg Island, this was the hardest. Of everything, this was the one thing she didn't want to believe or accept, harder even than believing her father could have betrayed his best friend so heinously.

She'd given Gabriele everything of herself and *it had all been a lie.*

Sharply pointed talons clawed at her heart, slashing into her belly, slicing great chunks out of her.

'I never lied to you.' He spoke calmly but his chest rose and fell rapidly, his strong nose flaring. 'The contract never said anything about me not continuing my fight to clear my name and finding the evidence to prove your father was behind the fraud.'

'You're lying to me now!' Her control failed her. She grabbed a pile of the papers and began ripping into them, wishing it were his flesh she was tearing into. 'You've been lying to me from the beginning. You knew damn well I thought it meant you would leave my father alone, that marrying you meant my family would be safe. God, I was starting to think you were someone special—I was prepared to have your baby! And you were lying to me and using me, you manipulative *bastard.*'

He yanked at his hair, his eyes black with feverish emotion. 'Goddammit, Elena, I spent two years in prison for a crime *your father* committed. My dad died of a broken heart and you've seen how my mother is with your own eyes—do you really think I could just let that go? Your father deserves to pay for those crimes.'

'If my father did it then yes, he *does* deserve to pay, but *I don't.* I have done nothing, not to you, not to your family, not to anyone.' Furious, heartbroken tears fell like a waterfall from her eyes. 'And you know that's true. You know I'm innocent but you couldn't give a damn, so long as you get your vengeance.'

The colour that had returned to his face paled again. 'Elena…'

'How much did you pay Carlos to turn traitor?' she screamed. 'How much are you paying him to lie for you?'

Sadness now rang from his eyes and he raised a hand as if to reach for her before dropping it back down to his side. 'It's not lies. It's the truth. That's all I ever wanted—for the truth to be told and my family's good name to be restored. But I swear to you, I didn't know you were innocent. I would never have involved you in any of this if I had.'

'And that's supposed to make it all right? As if I will *ever* believe another word that comes from your mouth.' She gave a maniacal laugh that ripped through her throat. 'I'm nothing but a pawn in your game and I will hate you for the rest of my life.'

She couldn't look at him, couldn't look at the lying mouth she had kissed with such love. Couldn't look in the eyes that had devoured her and made her feel so wanted and *necessary*.

It had all been a lie.

'Where are you going?' A trace of panic resonated from his voice.

Facing him for the last time, she said with all the loathing she muster, 'As far away from you and your ugly vendetta as I can get. I never want to see you again.'

The door slammed shut and she was gone.

Gabriele stared at the blank space where only a moment before Elena had stood, his heart pounding and nausea rising from his stomach to his throat.

Dear God, what had he done?

What had he done?

CHAPTER THIRTEEN

ELENA STOPPED LONG enough at Gabriele's apartment to get her passport and leave his car keys on the sideboard. Everything else could go to hell.

From Florence, she took a flight to Sweden, hired a car and headed for the sleepy town her mother had been raised in. She didn't think she had ever needed her more.

During the long drive she did not allow herself to think of Gabriele. As far as she was concerned, he didn't exist. She would spend the rest of her life scrubbing clean her memories of him if she had to.

Eventually she arrived at a large timber chalet on the edge of a lake.

She switched the engine off and gazed at it with a lump in her throat and an ache in her heart.

This was where her mother had spent her childhood. And here was the second-best thing to the woman who had given birth to her.

The front door opened and a tall white-blonde woman appeared, staring at the car with a quizzical expression.

Elena got out and gazed at her aunt.

'Elena?'

She tried to speak but the words wouldn't form.

Agnes must have seen something in her expression for concern flittered over her face and she hurried over to her. Instead of bombarding her with questions, her kindly aunt simply pulled her into an embrace and whispered into her hair, 'Oh, Elena, it is so wonderful to have you here.'

And with those words, Elena burst into tears.

Hours later Elena sat at a scrubbed wooden kitchen table drinking sweet tea. Her aunt had sent Henrick, her husband, out on errands, with the words, 'Don't hurry back.'

Elena told her everything. Every sordid detail.

Agnes didn't say much, seemingly content to listen and provide cakes and biscuits for the never-ending supply of tea.

'Do you think your father's involved?' was the first question she asked when Elena finished talking.

'I don't know,' Elena whispered. 'I know there are many things I've been kept in the dark about.'

For the first time she forced herself to really think about her father, not just as the man who had raised and loved her but as something else. Someone else. Someone who could be cruel enough to frame his best friend and allow his own godson to go to prison for a crime he himself had committed.

'Do *you* think he's capable of doing it?'

'If you had asked me that twenty-five years ago I would have said no,' Agnes answered matter-of-factly. 'But losing your mother…' She closed her eyes and shook her head. When she opened them to look at Elena, sadness emanated from them. 'Do you know much about your parents' marriage?'

'Not really.' She attempted a smile. 'I know they met when my mother was on holiday in Italy.'

Agnes returned the smile. 'They did. It was love at first sight for them both. They were smitten with each other. I had never seen Hilde so happy.'

'I'm sensing a "but" coming.'

Her aunt grimaced. 'Your father is a very possessive man. He couldn't bear to let her out of his sight. He hated her talking to other men.'

'He didn't…?' She couldn't bring herself to say the words.

'Hit her?' Agnes supplied. 'No. Never. But he never thought twice about beating up any man who disrespected her or who your father felt was getting too close to her. Hilde was a very gentle woman—it upset her very much.'

Elena couldn't think of anything to say to that. This was a side to her father she had never seen.

'I am telling you this so you can understand how your father became the man he is now,' Agnes said gently. 'They *were* happy. They loved each other very much. When your mother died…' She tapped the side of her head. 'I don't think he ever got over it. He threw a protective cloak around his children and hardened himself to the rest of the world. He loved his boys but you were always the apple of his eye. He doted on you. You were a fighting tomboy but you have your mother's gentle heart. I don't think your father could bear for you to see him as less than perfect.'

Elena put her hand to her throat and closed her eyes.

Trying to forget thoughts of disloyalty, and trying to think dispassionately about Gabriele when all she wanted to do was spend the rest of her life crying, she took a deep breath and mentally counted off some indisputable facts.

She ran the European division. It was the division where nothing creative happened. It was an outpost for selling stock. Nothing more. All the meat and bones of her father's company was conducted in Asia and South America. She had never travelled to either continent. She was kept ignorant of whatever happened there.

Alfredo Mantegna had been her father's best friend. When Alfredo had emigrated with his family to open his car empire to the North American market, her father had used Alfredo's new contacts to expand his own empire.

Her father no longer had any business dealings in North America.

A decade ago, her father and Alfredo had merged the overlapping parts of their two business entities into a new business that they owned fifty-fifty. The headquarters were based in Brazil, where her own father had plenty of businesses and where Alfredo had none. That business was proven to have been used as a front for fraud and money laundering. The trail had led to the Mantegnas.

Even through her loathing of Gabriele she could not believe he would be involved in something like that. Gabriele's mother...

Is he in prison yet?

Elena clamped a hand over her mouth and swallowed back the rising nausea.

'It is natural to want to see only the best in the people we love,' Agnes said in a quiet, sympathetic voice. 'You and your father have always been exceptionally close. If your father *was* behind it I am certain he would do everything in his power to protect you from it.'

'I need to talk to him, don't I?' Elena whispered.

Agnes nodded and reached across the table to take her hand. 'I suspect you're the only person who could ever get the truth from him.'

Elena blew out a long breath of air.

She'd buried her head in the sand for long enough.

She needed to speak to him face to face, now, before Gabriele and Carlos went to the FBI. If they hadn't already.

Her father answered his phone after the first ring and, while he hesitated at first, agreed to her request to meet her in Sweden.

He arrived at Agnes's cabin the very next day.

That he was still at liberty soothed her. It meant Gabriele knew his evidence wasn't strong enough, or the FBI had discounted it, or Carlos had changed his mind about being a turncoat.

She greeted him at the door and was immediately engulfed in a huge embrace.

'It's been many years since I've been in this house,' he said as she led him to the kitchen, where Agnes had laid out lunch for them. Clearly ill at ease, he craned his neck at every turn, looking at everything. 'What brought you here?'

'I wanted to see Aunt Agnes,' she said. 'Don't worry—they've gone out. It's just you and me.'

'Mantegna's not with you?'

She shook her head, taking a seat. 'I've left him.'

He paused, staring hard at her, then a smile spread across the tension-strewn face. 'If I had known that I would have brought champagne.'

She didn't respond, taking the lid off the casserole dish. Even if he'd magically produced a bottle of champagne she felt too heartsick to drink.

She didn't think her heart would ever beat normally again.

Why couldn't she forget him? Why was it that every time she closed her eyes, all she could see was Gabriele? After everything he'd done, why did she *ache* so much for him?

You would have done the same if you were in his shoes. If someone had destroyed your family the way Gabriele believes your father destroyed his, you would have stopped at nothing for revenge.

She would never have hurt an innocent though.

He didn't know you were innocent.

'So you have seen the light,' her father said, nodding his approval. 'I told your brothers, I said, "Don't worry about Elena, she's a good girl, she knows where her loyalty lies."'

She ladled some casserole into a bowl, holding it tightly to stop her shaking hands from spilling the hot liquid onto the table.

'Gabriele's loyalty is to his father,' she said, choosing her words with care.

Something flickered on her father's face.

And in that moment all her doubts crystallised and the truth came crashing down on her.

It was all true. All of it. Everything Gabriele had said. All true.

'Elena?'

She looked into her father's concerned face, the room swimming, darkness seeping into her pores, infecting her blood.

The truth was what her heart had been telling her for weeks but she had been too wilfully blind to see.

Gabriele tied a cufflink to his sleeve and smiled at his reflection.

It made no difference.

He still looked shot.

He tried again. This time his mouth wouldn't co-operate.

His driver was waiting outside for him. At Mantegna HQ, over two dozen media journalists were congregating for the launch of the new Alfredo car, along with over a hundred of the staff members who had worked most closely on it. Caterers had delivered enough canapés to feed an army and enough champagne to get a battalion drunk.

This was the culmination of the past year's hard work, a car made to honour his father, and he could no longer bring himself to care.

How could he ever care about anything when the best part of him wouldn't be by his side?

She would never be by his side again.

Having got increasingly frantic that Elena had seemingly dropped off the face of the earth, he'd hired a bunch of private detectives on all continents to find her. Just to satisfy him that she was well. Four hours ago he'd got the message that she'd landed in Rome.

The relief had been indescribable.

After five days of silence he at least had confirmation that she was alive.

She wouldn't see him. He knew that. She refused to answer his calls or his messages. His emails bounced back as undeliverable.

How could he stand up in front of one hundred and fifty people and make a speech when he couldn't think of a single thing to say that wasn't a plea for Elena to come back to him?

Why had he attempted to defend himself?

There was no defence for what he'd done and the more he tortured himself by thinking about it, the more he accepted how blinded and despicably wrong he'd been.

He could hear his housekeeper hovering behind his bedroom door, knew she wanted to remind him of the time and how late he was going to make the launch.

Instead of getting into gear, he slipped into Elena's dressing room.

All her clothes were still neatly hung up or folded away, as if waiting for her to return to claim them.

He knew she would never reclaim them.

He spotted the silver top she'd worn on their first night out together and pulled it off the hanger, burying his nose in it, hoping to catch her scent before it faded completely.

It had already gone.

A sharp burn at the backs of his eyes caught him. He blinked it away as a commotion outside caught his attention. Swaying slightly, he went back into his room and opened the door.

Anna Maria stood there, looking flushed.

'Have you seen the news?'

Elena's house was in a quiet, affluent street in Rome's Parioli district. Soft lights glowed behind the shuttered windows When Gabriele found the red door he was searching for, he put his hands to his knees and allowed himself to breathe.

It had been two hours since Anna Maria had shown him the coverage dominating the Italian news channels and, he suspected, the US ones too. In that time he'd commandeered a helicopter to fly him from Florence and taken the cab ride from hell across Rome's streets, which were only marginally better to drive through than Florence's. Ten minutes ago he'd thrown a hundred-euro bill at the driver and got out, figuring it had to be quicker walking.

Taking one last apprehensive breath, he climbed the steps and pressed the doorbell. He banged on the door for good measure too.

When there was no answer, he rang and banged again. He would ring and bang on the door all night if he had to.

After what was probably only a minute but felt much, much longer, he heard a clicking noise followed by the slow turning of the door handle.

The door opened a fraction and a green eye appeared in the gap.

'Elena…' He couldn't say anything more. His throat had closed up.

She didn't say anything, her mostly concealed face staring at him blankly as if a stranger were on her doorstep.

'Can I come in?' he asked hoarsely.

Still not speaking, she shook her head.

'Please? I will only take a minute of your time.'

Another shake of her head.

He bowed his head and exhaled heavily. 'I understand.'

He raised his head to look back at her. She had almost entirely closed the door. Only the tiniest of gaps remained open.

'I don't expect you to believe me but I had nothing to do with your father's arrest,' he said quietly, certain she was listening. 'I destroyed the evidence I had. I just wanted you to know that and to tell you that I'm sorrier than words can say for what I've done to you.'

He bowed his head again and swallowed.

He expected no response and none followed.

But she was still there, still listening.

Gabriele sank to the floor and pressed his cheek to the door. 'My father would be heartbroken if he knew what I'd done in his name. I forced you into a marriage you didn't want. I made you dress in clothes you didn't want. I made you sign a contract stating the only way you could leave was if my baby was in your belly. I took your virginity.' He sucked in a breath and gazed up at the starry night sky. 'I did all that for revenge against your father, not against you. But you were my pawn and I was going to play you—I *did* play you. I told myself that you *had* to be in league with your father, as if that could excuse what I was doing. But you were nothing like my prejudices expected. You were everything. You *are* everything. *My* everything. I fell in love with you, Elena, but I was so blinded by revenge I couldn't see it.'

Placing a palm against the door, he prayed she was still there, still listening to him.

'You told me once that there wouldn't be a minute of the day when I didn't regret what I'd done to you. Well, that day is here. I know you will never forgive me but I wanted you to know that I will never forgive myself either. You wanted to see me burn in hell and you have your wish; I'm there. Every day without you is agony.'

He pinched the bridge of his nose and blinked rapidly, then got to his feet. He'd said everything he wanted to say. Everything he could say.

Almost stumbling back down the steps on legs that felt filled with lead, he stood on the pavement not having a clue where to go.

Elena leaving him had left him rudderless.

'I know it wasn't you who had my father arrested.'

The hairs on the back of his neck stood on end.

He turned slowly.

Elena stood clinging to the open doorway. Her face was pinched, her hair loose but lank around her shoulders. All she wore was a pair of leggings and a long-sleeved baggy top.

'It was me.'

And then she was crying, her hand clasped over her

mouth, her face a stream of tears, her whole body trembling with the force of her misery.

He flew back up the steps and took hold of her, pulling her to him.

When she wrapped her arms around him and sobbed into his chest, he held her tight, devastated to see the depths of her despair.

This was all his fault.

She tilted her head back to look at him with red-rimmed eyes, tears still pouring down her cheeks.

'It was me,' she repeated, biting into her lip.

He brushed her tears away and gazed into her distraught face. 'What was you?'

'My father.' She hiccuped. 'I made him confess. I told him if he didn't he would never see me again.' Her face crumpled. 'Oh, Gabriele, I'm so sorry. He did frame your father and let you go to prison for it. He's been laundering money for years. You were right all along but I couldn't see it.'

Unable to bear her distress any longer, he pulled her back into his arms and stroked her hair. 'My love, please, no, you have nothing to apologise for.'

'I didn't believe you.'

'Of course you didn't. He's your father. We all want to believe the best of our parents.' He burrowed his nose in her hair, breathing her in, hardly able to believe she was allowing him to hold her and that she held him in turn.

'You should be at the launch,' she suddenly wailed. 'This was your big night for your father…'

'It doesn't matter,' he cut in. '*You* are all that matters. My father would understand.'

When she was finally still, he took her face in his hands and stared intently into her eyes. 'Elena…why? Why did you make him confess?'

Incredulity came into her eyes. 'Because what he did was despicable. What he did to you and your family…' She shook her head, her chest shuddering. 'I'm still struggling to believe he could do such a thing. The money laundering and fraud… I might have been able to accept that, but to set your family up like he did and watch you be imprisoned for it…'

Her entire body shook, fresh tears falling over his hands.

'He was jealous of your father's success. When my mother died his jealousy grew—he saw your father with a happy family and thriving business and it turned him. When he learned the FBI was monitoring him, he framed your father without any remorse. I'm trying to understand how he could do it but…' She blew a breath of air out. 'I can never forgive him for what he's done to you.'

'Listen to me,' he said, speaking quietly. 'Whatever he's done, he's still your father. You will always love him and he will always love you. Never forget that.'

'I feel tainted,' she whispered.

A dog barked from across the street, its walker staring at them with curiosity.

'Can we go inside and talk before someone accuses me of bothering you?' he asked.

She attempted a laugh. 'You want to come inside a Ricci house?'

'The Ricci blood can't be all bad if it made you.'

She gazed at him, her brow furrowed.

'Can't you see how special you are that your father would willingly go to prison rather than lose you?' He kissed her forehead. 'And you're so special to me that I ripped up the documents and sent Carlos on his way rather than have your father arrested because your happiness and peace of mind mean more to me than anything. More than revenge. More than clearing my name. I had lost all faith in humanity and you gave it back to me—you, the woman with Ricci blood in her veins. I love you more than I knew was possible and I will never, ever forgive myself for what I've done to you.'

'Your name *will* be cleared now,' she said softly.

'That means a lot to me,' he admitted. 'I'm just sorry it comes with such a heavy price for you.'

'I'll survive.' She swallowed and gazed into his eyes. 'I'll survive if you're with me.'

Speech suddenly became impossible.

Elena stared at the man she loved, wishing he could see into her heart and read what was there. 'You saved me.'

His eyes didn't leave her face.

'You saved me from those men and then you saved me from myself. You opened my eyes to who I really am. You taught me there's nothing to be ashamed of in being a woman; in being *me*.' She looked up at the starry sky. 'Without you in my life, it feels like all the stars have gone out.'

When she gazed back at him, stark, silent hope and disbelief were etched on his face.

Now it was her turn to touch *him*. She pressed her palm to his cheek, a shiver racing through her to feel the smooth skin she'd dreamed of every night since she'd left him.

'I love you, Gabriele, and I forgive you.'

His eyes widened and he nestled into her palm.

'You love me?' he asked in a choked voice. 'You *forgive* me?'

'What you did... I can't say in all honesty that I wouldn't have done the same in your shoes. What you've been through—what we've both been through...'

'If you give me a second chance I will never lie to you again,' he said, with such sincerity the last doubts in her heart fluttered away.

'I know,' she said softly.

Suddenly he dropped to one knee and took her hand. 'Elena Ricci, will you do me the honour of divorcing me?'

'What?'

A smile tugged at his lips, the heavy lines that had marred his face since his arrival on her doorstep lifting.

'Divorce me…and then do me the even greater honour of marrying me, but this time for real. I love you and I want to spend the rest of my life with you. I want to have little Mantegna and Ricci babies with you.'

If her heart could expand any further it would explode out of her chest.

All the misery of the past five days was pushed aside as a wave of joy ripped through her.

'So will you?' he asked, still on one knee, his finger rubbing the gold band on her wedding finger. 'Do you want it too?'

'More than anything,' she said, a beam she had no control over spreading over her face. 'I love you, Gabriele.'

With that, he pulled the ring off, threw it over his shoulder and kissed the space on her finger where it had been. Gazing back up into her eyes, he said, 'The next ring I put there will be for keeps. All the rings I put on this finger will be for keeps just as my heart is yours to keep for ever.'

'My heart belongs to you too and it always will.' She laughed, then planted the most enormous kiss she could muster on his welcoming mouth. 'Shall we go inside now?'

'Yes. Let's go and make some Mantegna-Ricci babies.'

And they did.

EPILOGUE

'YOU'RE GOING to be late,' Lisbeth squealed the second Elena stepped into the hotel bedroom. Lisbeth was already dressed in her mint bridesmaid dress.

'No, I'm not.'

Malin stuck her head out of the bathroom. 'You're here. Thank God. Your ex-husband has been driving us crazy.'

'He knew I was on my way back.'

'You didn't speak to him?' Lisbeth demanded. 'That's bad luck.'

'I'm sure it's only *seeing* them before the wedding that's bad luck.' Elena hid a grin. She swore her Swedish cousins had sucked all the nerves out of her and channelled them into themselves.

She herself had only felt mild anxiety at her journey taking an hour longer than anticipated. There was plenty of time. Besides, Gabriele would wait for her. He would always wait.

There was a bang on the door.

'Stay there,' Lisbeth hissed. 'It's probably your ex-husband.' She tugged the door open a fraction.

'Is she back?' came Gabriele's voice.

'Yes, she's here. Now go away. You can't see her.'

'How was her father?'

'He was good,' Elena called, ignoring the glares from her cousins. 'He's holding up well. Now go before Lisbeth and Malin spontaneously combust.'

She'd left before breakfast to visit her father at the prison he was being held at as he awaited sentencing. She couldn't get married without seeing him first. It had lifted her heart to hear him give them his blessing.

She visited him whenever she could. It would be easier after sentencing as he'd be transferred to a prison in Italy, so she'd be able to visit much more regularly.

He liked her visits. While she would never be able to forgive him for what he'd done to Gabriele and his family, she still loved him and he loved her. He must have taken a lesson in selflessness from her ex-husband as he'd completely exonerated her brothers from any blame. Unfortunately he hadn't been able to save them from financial ruin. That they still had roofs over their heads was entirely down to Gabriele.

Gabriele chuckled from the other side of the door. 'I'll see you in a couple of hours.'

A couple of hours?

From feeling as if she had all the time in the world, she suddenly saw the time with the same eyes as her panicking cousins.

In a flurry, she got herself into gear.

After she'd had a quick shower, Lisbeth and Malin got to work.

Her hair was dried and styled, her face made up and then it was time to get her into her dress.

When she was done she truly felt like a bride.

Her ivory dress, which hugged her figure, had a five-foot train. It sparkled and shimmered under the light. She could feel the rest of her shimmering with it.

The Somerset County church they were marrying in shimmered too, the autumn sunshine bouncing light off its white walls.

This was it. This was her wedding day. This was the day she committed the rest of her life to the man she loved.

With Aunt Agnes on her arm to walk her down the aisle and her cousins behind her, Elena took the first step towards Gabriele, her ex-husband and, any moment now, to be her husband for ever.

He stood at the front in his black tuxedo and did nothing but gaze at her adoringly as she walked towards him.

Elena beamed hugely to see his mother sitting beside Loretta in the family seats. It had been touch and go whether she would make it—it could only be feasible if she was having a good day—but they had decided to take the risk of marrying in Somerset County in the hope she would be well enough,

The gamble had paid off.

Finally they exchanged their vows and Gabriele was sliding a gold band onto her finger with their names and the date engraved on it so it rested above the diamond engagement ring he'd given her the day after they'd embraced the love they had.

And then they were pronounced man and wife. Gabriele and Elena Mantegna-Ricci.

The little life growing in her belly would get the best of them both.

* * * * *

If you enjoyed this story, check out
these other great reads from Michelle Smart
HELIOS CROWNS HIS MISTRESS
THESEUS DISCOVERS HIS HEIR
TALOS CLAIMS HIS VIRGIN
THE PERFECT CAZORLA WIFE
Available now!

Don't miss Lynne Graham's 100th book!
BOUGHT FOR THE GREEK'S REVENGE
Also available this month

MILLS & BOON®

MODERN™

POWER, PASSION AND IRRESISTIBLE TEMPTATION

Nikolai Drakos is determined to have his revenge against the
man who destroyed his sister. So stealing his enemy's
intended fiancé seems like the perfect solution! Until Nikolai
discovers that woman is Ella Davies...

*Read on for a tantalising excerpt from
Lynne Graham's 100th book,*

BOUGHT FOR THE GREEK'S REVENGE

'Mistress,' Nikolai slotted in cool as ice.

Shock had welded Ella's tongue to the roof of her mouth because
he was sexually propositioning her and nothing could have prepared
her for that. She wasn't drop-dead gorgeous... *he* was! Male heads
didn't swivel when Ella walked down the street because she had
neither the length of leg nor the curves usually deemed necessary
to attract such attention. Why on earth could he be making *her* such
an offer?

'But we don't even know each other,' she framed dazedly. 'You're
a stranger...'

'If you live with me I won't be a stranger for long,' Nikolai pointed out with monumental calm. And the very sound of that inhuman calm and cool forced her to flip round and settle distraught eyes on his lean darkly handsome face.

'You can't be serious about this!'

'I assure you that I am deadly serious. Move in and I'll forget your family's debts.'

'But it's a *crazy* idea!' she gasped.

'It's not crazy to me,' Nikolai asserted. 'When I want anything, I go after it hard and fast.'

Her lashes dipped. Did he want her like that? Enough to track her down, buy up her father's debts, and try and buy rights to her and her body along with those debts? The very idea of that made her dizzy and plunged her brain into even greater turmoil. 'It's immoral… it's blackmail.'

'It's definitely *not* blackmail. I'm giving you the benefit of a choice you didn't have before I came through that door,' Nikolai Drakos fielded with a glittering cool. 'That choice is yours to make.'

'Like hell it is!' Ella fired back. 'It's a complete cheat of a supposed offer!'

Nikolai sent her a gleaming sideways glance. 'No the real cheat was you kissing me the way you did last year and then saying no and acting as if I had grossly insulted you,' he murmured with lethal quietness.

'You *did* insult me!' Ella flung back, her cheeks hot as fire while she wondered if her refusal that night had started off his whole chain reaction. What else could possibly be driving him?

Nikolai straightened lazily as he opened the door. 'If you take offence that easily, maybe it's just as well that the answer is no.'

Visit **www.millsandboon.co.uk/lynnegraham**
to order yours!

MILLS & BOON®

0616_LG100P2

MILLS & BOON®

Mills & Boon have been at the heart of romance since 1908… and while the fashions may have changed, one thing remains the same: from pulse-pounding passion to the gentlest caress, we're always known how to bring romance alive.

Now, we're delighted to present you with these irresistible illustrations, inspired by the vintage glamour of our covers. So indulge your wildest dreams and unleash your imagination as we present the most iconic Mills & Boon moments of the last century.

Visit **www.millsandboon.co.uk/ArtofRomance** to order yours!